SPECIAL PREVIEW INSIDE THIS EDITION
of another Ann Burton tale of fiery passion, legend-
ary courage, breathtaking adventure, and heartrend-
ing betrayal . . .

Deborah's Story
August 2006

*Read an excerpt of this Women of the Bible novel in the
back of this book*

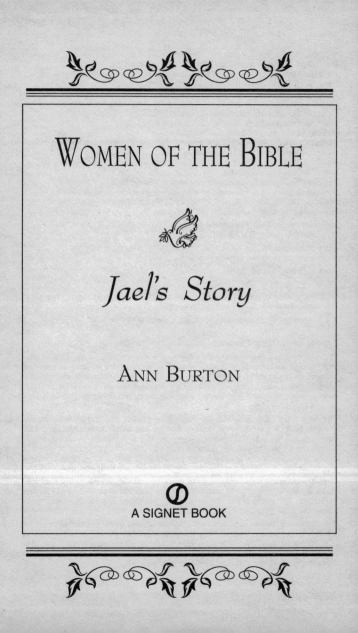

WOMEN OF THE BIBLE

Jael's Story

ANN BURTON

A SIGNET BOOK

SIGNET
Published by New American Library, a division of
Penguin Group (USA) Inc., 375 Hudson Street,
New York, New York 10014, USA
Penguin Group (Canada), 90 Eglinton Avenue East, Suite 700, Toronto,
Ontario M4P 2Y3, Canada (a division of Pearson Penguin Canada Inc.)
Penguin Books Ltd., 80 Strand, London WC2R 0RL, England
Penguin Ireland, 25 St. Stephen's Green, Dublin 2,
Ireland (a division of Penguin Books Ltd.)
Penguin Group (Australia), 250 Camberwell Road, Camberwell, Victoria 3124,
Australia (a division of Pearson Australia Group Pty. Ltd.)
Penguin Books India Pvt. Ltd., 11 Community Centre, Panchsheel Park,
New Delhi - 110 017, India
Penguin Group (NZ), cnr Airborne and Rosedale Roads, Albany,
Auckland 1310, New Zealand (a division of Pearson New Zealand Ltd.)
Penguin Books (South Africa) (Pty.) Ltd., 24 Sturdee Avenue,
Rosebank, Johannesburg 2196, South Africa

Penguin Books Ltd., Registered Offices:
80 Strand, London WC2R 0RL, England

First published by Signet, an imprint of New American Library,
a division of Penguin Group (USA) Inc.

First Printing, March 2006
10   9   8   7   6   5   4   3   2   1

*To my wonderful and brilliant friend Sheila,
whose expertise and encouragement
made this book a sheer joy to write.*

CHAPTER

1

I stepped out of the bride's tent, accompanied by my father and my brother, to the sound of clashing tambourines and the high melody of the flutes—as well as to the racing of my own heart. My fingers tightened around my father's arm. I walked forward to meet for the first time the man to whom I would be given as wife.

We were all gathered—my family and friends, our neighbors, and my soon-to-be-husband's family, including his other wife and many of his sons—at the high shrine of Baal on Mount Tabor, to beseech the god whose rains brought fertility to the earth to bring the same fertility to our union. Such is the custom of Canaanites, who are my people. And the Kenite Heber had adopted our customs as his own. This, both my mother and my father told me, would be a good thing: I could keep my house idols; I could worship my own gods; I would share my husband with another wife who was Canaanite like me.

My family was pleased that they had arranged such a favorable match for me. "He's a close friend of King Jabin," my father said, "and of Jabin's great general, Sisera. Heber has the trust of the two most powerful men in Hazor."

"He is rich," my mother said. "He will give you fine clothes, and jewelry, and good food to eat. In his care, you will not want for anything."

Heber had paid my bride-price extravagantly, as befitted a man of his wealth; he had given my father a matched pair of oxen, both young, strong, and healthy, and a cast Baal of solid silver that he had made with his own hands. My father declared the oxen extraordinary, while my mother praised the exquisite workmanship of the little idol.

"You are marrying a man of means," my younger sister said with envy in her voice. "And a man whose other wife, and even whose concubine, has borne him strong sons." She said I could count on the blessings of Baal to give me sons.

In every way, I clearly faced a fine future. The augur had foretold for me many strong sons by Heber, and much happiness in his household. The morning was cool and bright, befitting the season, the sky clear, the witnesses happy, the revelry waiting to begin. I could not offer up a single complaint or a single reason to worry; my parents had worked to give me the best future possible.

Why then did my heart race like a whipped horse?

I hid within my veils and prayed to each god or goddess who might help me—to Father El the Bull, Mother Asherah the Serpent of the Sea, Anat the Maiden, Ashtartu the Divine Nymph. I prayed that Heber would be good and kind and gentle. That he would look at me warmly and with pleasure, that he would welcome me as a companion, that he would give me both sons and daughters. I prayed that he might be fair to look upon, though I was quick to offer up fairness of face and form in exchange for goodness of spirit.

I leaned upon my father's arm for guidance as we made our way to the altar that stood between the bride's tent and the groom's tent. The veils over my face so blinded me that I could make out only barest shapes, only those borders where dark gave way to light, or light to dark. I stumbled, and my father made a soothing sound and kept me on my feet.

"Not much farther, then," he said. "Steady, Daughter, and your impatience will be rewarded."

I felt some little impatience, it was true, but far more than that, I felt the fear of a woman waiting to catch a glimpse—for the first time—of the man who would be her husband and master for the rest of her life. If my parents thought well of Heber, I could draw hope from that. But only so much hope, for they would not be leaving all they knew to live with

3

strangers in a place far from the strong walls of Hazor. They would not make their lives in his tent, nor would they share his bed.

I reached the altar at last, and Baal's priest raised his hands in the air. The music stopped, and a hush fell over the sacred ground. The ceremony started. I had been a wedding guest before; I knew the way of the ceremony. The incense, the prayers, the ask-and-answer of the vows, the sacrifice to Baal asking the blessing of children, and then the lifting of the veil that would let us see each other for the first time.

He was older than I had hoped, with a strong hooked nose, straight brows, and a mouth that curled slightly at the corners in some silent amusement as he looked at me. His hair, long and thin at the top, was going to gray at the temples, his square-cut beard with its braids down both sides was already almost entirely gray.

He was a tree of a man, broad of shoulder and sinewy of arm, as befitted a smith who spent most of his days working with the iron of war chariots and the bronze and iron of armor and swords. But his belly was round and full and deep; he clearly did not go hungry.

I wanted to look at him and feel the yearnings so often described in the songs of Ashtartu. I wanted to feel my blood quicken and my body soften in readiness of his embrace. I wanted to feel joy that he was my husband. I wanted some stirring of love in my heart, or even to think that I might like him. That he and I might hope for happiness together.

But that curling at the corners of his mouth looked cruel to me. And the narrowing of his eyes as he sized me up—a look I had seen in men enumerating the good and bad points of a cow or ewe or mare they were buying—sent a tiny arrow of dread into my heart. This was a mistake, I wanted to tell my father and my mother. I was not yet ready to marry.

But I was already so old. I was nineteen, and had been old enough for a husband at fifteen. My parents had turned away other offers for me because the men had been too poor, or not well established in trades, or foreign. They had waited to find a good husband for me.

And this man, Heber, was the best husband I could hope for. I was not a king's daughter, or the daughter of a general or a priest, I could not hope to find myself married to a shar, a prince. I was the daughter of craftsmen—weavers and dyers—and my parents could be proud that they had done so well for me. Even I had to think that the price of matched oxen and a silver house-idol in exchange for a woman who would be a second wife was extravagant.

When the priest declared us married, the music started up again, so loudly this time, I almost could not hear myself think. Everyone danced first, and drank wine, and feasted. And then we danced some more—this time the waypassehu, the traditional leaping dance of Baal, where the women's circle started separate from the men's circle, and the men's circle began around the altar. Then one woman broke the chain and led all the women into the center of the men's circle. Finally, Heber and I were pushed into the center of the two circles that spun in two directions, up against Baal's altar, where we, too, became symbolic offerings. Everyone was laughing and shouting, with the remarks becoming increasingly lewd, until at last both circles flew apart, and Heber tossed me over his shoulder, as grooms so often did, and ran with me to the groom's tent and pulled the flap shut. Outside, the merriment continued, becoming louder, though I would have thought no such thing possible.

Inside the tent, the noise was present, but so was a strange sense of silence. Heber laughed as he put me down on the floor, and I could see that a raised bridal bed had been made for us of mats put on a pedestal and covered with a white linen sheet. Staring at that bed and that white sheet, it seemed to me that all the world outside the tent fell away, leaving only the two of us, and the uncomfortable space between and around us.

Still chuckling, Heber turned his attention to me. "Well, girl—undress. Let me see what I bought for such a remarkable sum."

My heart hammered so hard, I thought it might come apart, and my breath clogged in my throat.

This was the part of the ceremony that some brides revel in, and others dread. Every married woman willing to tell me about what passed inside the groom's tent had a different story to tell, so that when I had heard as much as my ears could bear, I knew a great deal more about how things were between men and women. But I still had no idea how they would be for me.

I started fumbling with the layers of my wedding robes, though my hands were trembling and I had a difficult time of it. Heber's amused expression quickly turned to exasperation, and he grabbed me, untied my embroidered hagora—the sash that held my beautiful red wool kuttonet in place. He ripped the kuttonet off me and threw it across the tent without a second glance. Naked—I, who had never been seen undressed by any man before. I covered my breasts with my hands and stood before him. A smile reappeared on his face, the toothy smile of the jackal, and he stared at me.

I waited for some tender touch, some gentle embrace that would comfort me and soothe my fears, as in the songs of Ashtartu, but Heber was full of wine and lust. He pulled his own clothing off with no more ceremony than he'd used removing mine, and shoved me onto the bed.

And with no more care than a stallion takes a mare, and with just as much roughness, he took me.

It hurt, and I cried out in pain, and when he was

finished with me, I lay sobbing beneath him. He gave me a look of disgust, so that I turned my face away from him in shame.

"Enough of your noises, girl," he told me. He slapped me across the face and pushed me to my feet so that he could get at the blood-covered wedding sheet beneath us. He pulled on his robe, for according to custom, he would hang the sheet outside the tent to prove my virginity, and his virility.

"I'll have planted you with a nice fat baby boy from my efforts," he said. And then he laughed, and it was an ugly laugh. "You'll scream more when he comes out than you did when I went in." He tucked the sheet under his arm and walked to the tent flap, and then he turned for just a moment and looked back at me. "My other wife and my concubine will come and retrieve you. You ridiculous, whimpering embarrassment of a girl—stop your sobbing. You've served as women are supposed to serve. Now be quiet about it." I stood there, naked and bloody, and hung my head. "My women will make you presentable and talk some sense into you. Meanwhile, I've had enough of women for a while."

He left, and I threw myself onto that horrible bed and rolled into a ball. I lay there, rocking back and forth, weeping from shame and humiliation as much as from the pain.

After a while, two older women came into the tent. They spoke to me, though I did not truly hear what they said, and at last, with sighs and shakes of their heads, they stood me on my feet, and dressed me as they would have dressed a small child, and led me from the groom's tent.

Thus was it that I, Jael the Canaanite, daughter of Ummiar, became Jael the Kenite, wife of Heber.

CHAPTER
2

"**D**o you suppose she ever plans to wake up?"
I heard laughter, and a young woman's
voice saying, "Heber bought himself a lazy wife."

An older voice replied, the tone almost stern. "You
don't know how it was for her. She had never had
another man when he took her, Talliya. She didn't
come to him from having been one of Ashtartu's sacred prostitutes."

"Think you it was a pleasure to be presented at
Ashtartu's altar when I was fifteen, instructed to give
myself willingly to whomsoever would have me, and
to be taken by all who waited for a turn?"

And the older voice said, "I would think it was no
pleasure at all. But perhaps you ought to *remember*
that first time, and remind yourself that *her* first time
was with Heber. How much worse could the business be than that?"

The younger voice, which apparently belonged to
Talliya, once a servant of Ashtartu, said, "I cannot

deny the truth of *those* words." In her voice, I heard rueful laughter.

I opened my eyes and found myself in the women's half of an enormous tent. Two little boys played on the floor, one barely crawling and the other sturdily trudging. Two women watched them—the older worked with a loom and shuttle, weaving bright red cloth.

I lay looking around me for a few moments. This would be the first time that I would get to spend the day in Heber's tent, rather than trailing the camel that carried it, and the handful of goats and kids that Heber's beardless sons led. And I was from Hazor, where houses had solid walls and roofs, and no one moved them anywhere.

The tent was of goat hair, the cloth spread over a heavy wooden frame of posts and crossbeams. It was, to my eyes, immense—it had more space in it than had my parents' home back in Hazor. The roof was woven of dark brown goat-hair yarn, heavy spun. The sides had been woven in geometric patterns of brown and cream and red and gold; they were designed to be tied up during the day and rolled down at night or when bad weather threatened or privacy was necessary—all save the central panels, which divided the women's half from the men's.

From the posts over my head hung mallets and extra tent pegs, cook pots and herbs and a loom for weaving, skeins of spun yarn, dyed and undyed, and

11

net bags of wool and goat hair and flax, as well as skin bags of curdling milk. Along the central section of the wall between men's and women's sides, large pottery jars held water and grain and other food-stuffs. The straw-filled mattresses, save only mine, were already rolled up on the left side of the wall, neatly stacked.

The right side of that central wall formed a pass-through between men's and women's sides, though it was closed. I could see gaps between some of the panels, though, and thought it likely the women would peer through them to see what went on in the other half of the tent. The women's side of the tent held shrines to the goddesses Asherah, Anat, and Ashtartu.

It was a pretty, cozy place, warm against the cold morning air of late winter.

I was not happy to be there.

I sat up. I hurt—every muscle and every joint. I was not used to long walking; I'd been born in Hazor, and had lived all my nineteen years there with no reason to travel farther than to the well and sometimes to the outside of the city walls to one of the gods' holy places.

So it was that, having spent two days on my feet traveling from Hazor to the main camp of Heber's clan of Kenites, I remembered only vaguely my arrival at Heber's grand tent; we had walked the last bit of our journey in the dark. I had walked weeping some of the way, which is in itself a tiring thing; I knew, even as I hugged my mother and father good-bye, that I did not want to leave their home for that of my husband.

I had no doubt been tiresome. I had spoken to no one during the whole journey; I had simply mourned the loss of my parents and my sisters and brothers, sobbing as I walked and wishing that I could run home to my mother and not be caught. And yet the eyes of the women in Heber's tent now looked back at me with interest and compassion. These women, Heber's other wife and his concubine, would take the place of my sisters.

"So you have awakened at last," said the older of them, the weaver.

I nodded.

"I am Pigat, Heber's first wife. Welcome to our home—all that is ours is yours." She came over to me and kissed both my cheeks, then held my hands and smiled at me. And for a mercy, her smile was real. She had lines at the corners of her eyes, and her hair was the gray of iron, pulled back tightly and knotted at her neck. I would have guessed her near the age of my mother, though she was sturdy where my mother was slender, and fair where my mother was sun-browned. Her kuttonet, draped over her left shoulder and leaving the right bare, was of wheat-gold wool, finely woven and beautifully embroidered. Her simla—her cloak by day and her blanket

13

by night, wrapped around her shoulders, keeping her warm as she wove. The gold bracelets at her wrists jangled, and she wore gold at her ankles and around her neck, in hoops dangling from her ears, and in a lovely band at her forehead. She was clearly a rich woman, and well cared for—which was precisely the future my parents had hoped to secure for me.

Leaning against one of the tent posts, where she had been staring out from the cool dimness into the bright light beyond, stood a beautiful woman a handful of years younger than Pigat. Dressed all in green, she had rimmed her eyes with kohl and the green powder of malachite; and she wore jangling gold at her ears and throat. She flashed me a quick smile, and I saw that she had the most perfect teeth I had ever seen, even and very white and almost unworn by time. About her eyes and brows, and in the curve of her mouth, I thought I noted a likeness to Pigat. She said, "I'm Talliya, Heber's concubine," with a quiet amusement that surprised me; concubines had no easy life, I had been told. But Talliya seemed no less cared for than the woman who was Heber's wife. Her clothes were no less fine, her jewelry no poorer, even if she did wear less of it. She had picked up the crawling boy and put him to her breast.

I nodded, intimidated by both of them. I was the least of them. Neither old and powerful, nor elegant and beautiful and with a fine, fat baby at my breast, I discovered that I was exactly as my husband had described me—a foolish, weeping child. More than once on our long journey back to Heber's camp, which lay north of Mount Tabor, he had berated me for my behavior and for failing to give him pleasure. I had promised I would learn to do as he wished, but I did not know if I could please him.

"I'm Jael," I told them. "Second wife." I could hear the dismay in my own voice as I said those words, just as I could hear the self-pity. I knew they could hear it, too. I sat up and said, "I'm sorry for my manner. I had thought . . ." I clasped my hands together tightly and stared at them. "The wedding was not what I had expected, nor was my husband." And then I dared to look up at them. "But when I am a better wife, I know he will be a better husband."

Both women exchanged glances, then burst out laughing. Their laughter started as chuckles, but every time they looked at each other, they laughed harder, until Talliya clutched her sides and Pigat wiped the tears from her eyes with the back of her hand and leaned back in her chair, breathing as if she had run all the way to the Sea of Galilee.

"No, no," Pigat said, struggling to keep her voice low as she said it. "No, he will still be a terrible husband. He's . . ." She looked at Talliya and said, "Oh, dearest child, you must not think he is much husband at all, for all that he is a good smith."

"And a powerful man," said Talliya. "Not a man you want to anger, or let down."

Both women nodded. Pigat put aside her weaving, rose, and walked to the cloth wall that separated the men's side of the tent from the women's. She pushed aside the flap just enough to peek through. Apparently satisfied, she let it fall back into place and returned to her loom, settling into her weaving again.

I was stunned. I knew nothing of men; my parents had taken great care that I guard my virtue before my marriage. So I could not say of Heber that he was either a good husband or a bad one. All I could have said, if I dared even that much—and I did not— was that he frightened me, and that I didn't like him.

"He is not . . . as all husbands are?"

Talliya said, "He is not as all men are. In my service to Ashtartu, before I was sold to Heber, I had the knowing of uncounted men. Of them, Heber is surely the least skilled, coarsest, and vilest bull in the pasture."

"Oh." I sat considering that a man could be rich and keep the company of powerful men, and still earn mocking laughter and disdain from his women.

Pigat seemed to sense my unease, for she said, "We never want for anything, Jael. In the other duties of the husband, he is as he should be. We have good food, good clothes, a protected place in which to live. You need not worry about those things."

"But do not look to him for gentleness or kindness, or such pleasuring as men and women may find together," Talliya said. "He has none of those qualities in him."

"But I did not please him," I said. "He told me so. If he did not please me, that is of no matter to anyone but me—but if I do not please him—?" I closed my eyes against my remembered shame. "What am I to do so that he will not beat me? Or shout at me? Or hurt me the way he did before?" I opened my eyes and looked up at them. "Or cast me aside?"

Pigat beckoned me over, an expression of deep concern on her face. "The problem is a greater one than you might suspect, little sister. And in the cure for the problem lies a danger that could cost you your life, or us ours." Talliya crossed the tent to take a place next to Pigat, and suddenly it seemed quiet in the tent. They were watching me with wary eyes. "I can tell you what you can do that will spare you our lord's beatings, and his wrath, but if I tell you, I give not just my life, but Talliya's, and the lives of all our sons, into your hands."

I looked at each of them. I could see no humor in their eyes, nor any sign that they might be teasing me. I had to believe, looking at them, that they were serious, and that Pigat knew a secret that could be the death of all of us.

"You have to swear," Talliya said, "on all the gods and your own life, that you will never betray us.

And you have to know that if you do, we'll kill you before Heber has a chance to kill us."

Did I want to know something that terrible? Did I want to have a secret so dark hidden in my heart? I did not.

"If I know this secret, Heber will not beat me? Or hurt me?"

"Provided you are not barren," Pigat said, "this secret will save you all the pain and shame you will otherwise suffer with from this day until the day you die."

I knotted my hands in my robe, twisting the fabric, wishing again that I were safe in my father's house. I closed my eyes as if I could wish myself home again—but when I opened them, I was still in Heber's tent, far from Hazor. So I made my decision. I did not wish to spend my whole life being beaten. I had never been beaten in my father's house, and I had not cared for the experience in my husband's. I could keep a secret; I was no gossip. I had ever held confidences to my heart when my sisters or our friends gave them to me.

So I said, "I swear upon El and Asherah, upon Anat and Ashtartu, that all you tell me I shall keep in my heart, and never on my lips. Or Mot of All Deaths take me."

"Heber wants sons," Pigat said. As if his wanting were some terrible thing, and not what all men wanted. I nodded, hoping that this was not the secret for which I had sworn my life's blood. "Yet his seed is worthless—it gives nothing, it has no life in it, and no babies come from it. He is a dry stalk. I spent the first years of our marriage being beaten each month when I returned from the cleansing tent at the end of my time, because I had failed to conceive. I thought I was barren, and so I went each month to the shrine of Baal and prayed that Baal would grant me a son. And after two years of listening to me pray, the young priest there told me that, if I asked of him to make a special offering to Baal with me, Baal might grant me a baby."

She stared down at the hands that lay idle in her lap. "I did not know what else to do, so I asked the young priest to make this special offering with me. He took me behind the altar and did with me as Heber does—save only that he did not hurt me. And when he was done, Baal granted to me my son. The first of many, and that one sacrificed in Baal's fires in offering of thanks for Baal's generosity. But even after my firstborn died, Baal would be generous only after the priest and I made the special offering behind the altar."

Talliya spoke. "It has been the same for me. Pigat is right—Heber is a dried stalk. He does as he will, with never a moment when we think we might have conceived. When he begins to grow angry at our slowness to bear him sons, we go to the priest, whose name is Keret, and from him we take away sons that we present to Heber as his own."

"As for me," Pigat said, "when I wearied of Heber's attentions, I told him that my childbearing years had passed. He did his best to prove me wrong, but since I had ceased making my special offerings before Baal with Keret, at last Heber conceded that I had become an elder. And now he leaves me alone. My four strong sons work the smithy with him, and for them I have earned a place of honor in this house. Now I weave and make bread, and sleep wonderfully alone each night."

"I have borne five sons for Heber," Talliya said. "The littlest will be my last. I nearly died in childbirth with him. So I will go no more to make the offering with Keret the priest of Baal."

She nodded to the sweet-faced baby in her arms. His older brother was the toddler who sat digging up the dirt floor with a shell, playing quietly to the side of the rugs upon which Pigat, Talliya, and I sat. "I am done bearing children. So the burden falls on you, and on your courage to approach Keret."

I looked at both of them in turn, and I began to shake. "I could be stoned. *You* could be . . . stoned."

They each nodded.

"We could be killed and your sons sacrificed."

Pigat said, "Or we could be beaten for our barrenness, for shaming Heber by not giving him sons, and one day we could find ourselves put aside, divorced, and left to fend for ourselves. Even if I sat veiled at the gates of a city, I'm too old to think any man would pay me as his whore. Nor could I serve Ashtartu—the temples prefer young girls. My father and mother are long dead, and would never have given shelter to a divorced woman, in any case. I could only bring shame upon the houses of my brothers or sisters." She shrugged. "We are women. We are born in bitterness, and we die in bitterness. What would you have me do?" Her voice got even softer. "More important, what will you do?"

What would I do?

I hung my head. Women who betrayed their husbands by lying with other men were stoned to death. I knew this. I have never thrown the stones. Stoning is the right and duty of men. But I had seen the women buried to the waist in the street, begging for mercy, clutching at the hems of the robes of their husbands and their fathers and their brothers and their sons, while the men picked up stones against them, and with the priests and the other men of Hazor, battered those women until they lay, bloody and broken and still, in the middle of a mound of rocks.

And Heber's other women were telling me that not only had they shamed Heber by taking another man into their bodies, but that if I would please Heber with the strong sons he so desired, and spare myself beatings, I would have to do the same.

I looked at them, imagining these kind, quiet women in the eye of my mind being dragged into a cleared space in the camp. I could see Talliya with her babe at her breast, throwing her hands over him to protect him; I could hear Pigat begging Heber to spare them.

And I could see Heber's face, and it was not a face that would soften with mercy.

He would throw the first stone, and as many after as he could lift.

At them. At me.

I tried to see my way out of the trap into which I had been cast. Outside, one of Heber's beardless sons called that he had brought straw and twigs for our fire, and Pigat rose and went outside to gather them.

CHAPTER

3

A month I had lived in my husband's tent, in which most nights he took me to his bed, and I kept myself from crying by forcing myself to remember what would happen if I did. But my silence pleased him no more than my tears, and still he shouted at me or slapped me, and always told me I was worthless.

Days were better, for by day I had the companionship and friendship of my new sisters, and they had known my hurt, and knew as well the easing of it. We shared work: preparing food, weaving and sewing and mending, tending the two boys, carrying water, and dyeing and spinning. In work I found great comfort, for nothing more fully frees the mind from worry and pain than doing something necessary. And we shared the songs we sang in the tent as we worked, and the tales we told to each other, and our laughter.

Early one morning I rose and gathered our water

jars to take to the well, for I was youngest and strongest, and without a child who needed my attention. The four pretty clay kaddim, decorated with graceful birds in red and black, I set in a neat row. I liked them; we had the same sort of jars in my parents' home, painted with similar birds in red and black. I would need to make four trips to the well, for I could carry only one of the jugs at a time. Empty, they are quite light. Full, they are such a burden, I feel like an ill-used ox, and sometimes, balancing one on my head, I think I might be crushed beneath the weight of it. But I did yearn to leave early for my own reasons, too. Several other young wives would be at the well at daybreak, drawing their water for the day, and if I got there while they were there, they told stories about their lives as new wives that made me laugh. I talked sometimes about Talliya and Pigat to them, but never spoke of my husband.

My mother always said, "Kind words spread outward like ripples on water, but ill words follow you home." I had no wish to be followed home by any ill words I might say about my husband.

But as I was lifting the tent flap, I heard Heber outside, arguing with a man whose voice I had never heard before. It was a rich, deep voice, and managed to be both calm and angry.

I did not step out, but stood there, a water jug in my arms, and listened.

"I have already paid you, and you promised me

that you would have my sword ready for me this day!"

I peeked out the flap to see my husband standing next to his forge, facing a stranger, his face dark with anger. "I am pressed to the working of iron for a king. Who are you that you would demand of me that I set aside the king's iron sword, that I could make your bronze one?"

The young man flushed. He was, I thought, quite handsome. His black hair hung long and thick and curling, pulled back to the nape of his neck; his flashing eyes were black as anthracite, his nose strong, his mouth firm and well shaped. He had a young man's leanness, too, with broad shoulders and a tapering waist and sturdy, finely muscled legs. His was a young man's beard, not yet the long, thick beard of an elder, and his robes were white, and fringed in blue in the Israelite fashion.

"I am Levi of Kadesh, and I know only that I am not a king, but I paid you long months ago for a new sword. And that the last time I came to take ownership of it, you told me it was not yet ready, but that it would be ready today. I know, too, that a man's word is his word, whether he gives it to a king or a common soldier."

"Whereas," my husband told him, "I know that a man who keeps a king waiting while he forges a common soldier's sword is a man who in the king's sword will be forging the means to his own death."

"From olive harvest to the planting of the grain I have waited. Four long months in their season, and once each month I have traveled at your behest to claim that which I am rightfully owed. From olive harvest to the planting of the grain, you have each time turned me away with an excuse, so that I must believe you will never have time for my sword, though you had time enough to take my silver. Will you, then, repay the sixty shekels of silver I have paid you for the sword you promised?"

"I have not had a moment to myself," I heard my husband lie. "I work from sunup to sundown, in backbreaking labor, and though I would not expect you to know it, the forging of an iron sword is an art near enough to magic that there can be little difference. The metal must be heated and hammered and folded and hammered and heated and hammered again, day after day, with each day's work bringing the metal closer to true. And I have the knowing of the art; on the fingers of one hand could I give you the men who know it near as well as I, and on no fingers at all could I give you the men who know it better! You wanted a sword made by a master? Well, you'll get one, but by all the gods and Baal first, you'll get it in your turn, and not before."

To which the young man sighed and turned away.

My husband might have worked from sunup to sundown some days. He was a busy man. But I knew as well as I knew my own name that he was making a number of bronze swords right then. He was making them for men from the army of Jabin, and for friends of Jabin's general Sisera—but he was not at that moment making any iron swords, for Jabin or anyone else.

I turned to look at Pigat, who had come to stand beside me, as interested in what transpired on the other side of the tent as I was.

"Why did he say those things?" I whispered.

"You mean why did he lie?" Pigat laughed softly. "Because it suited him. The man is an Israelite. The Kenites have maintained their neutrality in this long war between Canaanites and Israelites because it's good for business to sell their smithing to both sides. But in the end, the Canaanites hold the fertile lowlands, and have the chariots and armies and wealth to keep the upstart Israelites confined to their poor highlands. So if Heber can take the man's silver, then keep him dangling like a hooked fish for his own amusement, he will. You'll hear him laughing about this tonight with his friends. They all do the same thing to some extent: they'll work for any who will pay them, because all silver spends the same. But they know, too, which goat gives the most milk."

"That's not right," I said.

"No. Of course not." Pigat shrugged. "But who are we to question those things our husband does? We are not smiths. We do not fashion metal, nor do we deal daily with men of high rank. Women have no place in the dealings of men."

I looked at her with curiosity. Pigat had, in one week, demonstrated to me that she held opinions on every subject under the sun, and that far from being the quiet and submissive woman I had thought her at our first meeting, she used every means at her disposal—flattery and wile and wit and guile and outright manipulation—to influence Heber when she thought the issue was one that mattered.

I had watched her with some admiration; she was not a woman who accepted no as an answer, just as a starting point. And most times she didn't even ask the question. "It's simpler," she told me early on, "if he thinks what he does is his own idea, whether it is to trade for more wool for the weaving, or to have new sandals made for all of us, or to lay in more wheat." She smiled a little. "He's very proud that he provides for us in such style—that he has more than one woman in his tent and that we are the first women in the camp with anything that is new or good."

The trick was, she said, never to let Heber find out that we were the ones bending him to our wills.

My husband's dishonesty with this soldier whose money he had taken was, I thought, something that mattered. I could not say for certain why it mattered to *me*.

If I closed my eyes, I could hear my father saying,

"Not the promises he makes, but the promises he keeps, are the measure of the man."

Then, my mother would look at my sisters and me and say, "Honor is a luxury of men; women cannot afford it."

Were my husband found to be dishonorable in his dealings, though, my sister-wives and I would suffer just as surely as he did. If men no longer bought from him, would we not share in his poverty? If he had no tent in which to sleep, would not the sky be our roof and the stones our beds, as well?

Honor might be a luxury of men, but lack of honor could be the punishment of women all the same.

Neither Pigat nor Talliya thought the matter of any importance to them. But I did. And does not the one who sees the rat in the grain kill it?

This was my rat, though I did not know how I might hope to kill the beast.

I lifted up the jar I had let slide to the floor while I listened to Heber, and went out into the morning air. Lost in thought, I made my way through the maze of clustered tents to the community well. It was a fine morning—still cool, with the sky clear and bright and the shadows long, and I imagined myself a child again, carrying a jug as I walked beside my mother to the well near their home. She and I would sing the songs she had sung as a girl as we walked.

I found myself singing the song of the dove and the calf.

> *The calf in the pen*
> *Cries woe, woe, woe,*
> *To the butcher and the slaughter,*
> *He'll go, go, go.*

I walked past the rug maker's tent, and saw his wife already out making bread for the day. She sat cross-legged on a stone, with her kneading stone before her, spinning the dough in her hands into flat cakes and throwing them down and into her tannur, her beehive-shaped bread oven, so that they stuck to the sides. I admired the sharp economy of her movements: the quick patting of her hands, the sharp snap of her wrist as she tossed the bread, the deft spearing of the finished bread with her bread staff, the matteh-lehem. We exchanged smiles as I went past, singing, and as we did, her grandchildren darted around me, carrying more straw and twigs to pile against the fire outside of the oven.

> *And the dove on the wing*
> *Sobs free, free, free,*
> *And flies to the top*
> *Of the tree, tree, tree.*

Outside Baal's tent, Keret the old priest and Jonin the young priest were lugging an enormous jug of curdled milk between them. I had heard Pigat say they made their own cheese, but I had never before seen proof of it. The young priest ignored me, but Keret smiled at me and gave me a wink as I passed by. I suppose he knew I was one of Heber's wives.

> *The calf bawls, Why*
> *Don't I have wings to fly*
> *Like the dove, like the dove,*
> *In the sky, sky, sky?*

Ajerash, who Talliya said was the best smith in our camp next to Heber, though he did no work with iron, was already hard at work. His sons were fueling his mosa, or smelter, and working a small bellows to make the flames hotter, while Ajerash heated bronze to pour into blade molds that lay in a neat row to one side of him. The bloodred metal glowed, soon to be liquid, and even from a distance the heat pushed me back. I could not imagine how smiths did what they did, day after day.

> *Run away, run away,*
> *Run away, my love,*
> *You can be the calf*
> *Or you can be the dove.*

I reached the little square that surrounded the well. Tall, graceful terebinth and broad evergreen oaks shaded the square. One of the oaks held a shrine to Asherah. I bent a knee as I passed, but my sister-wives and I would need water to do the work of the day, and if I dallied any longer, I would make myself a stumbling block to all of us.

> *When the sorrows come,*
> *You can cry, cry, cry,*
> *Or take up your wings*
> *And fly, fly, fly.*

At the well, I put down the jugs on the damp earth. The other young wives had already come and gone. Just as well, I thought. It would give me time to think.

"I would guess you more a dove than a calf," a deep voice said just behind me. "You sing like a sad little bird."

I jumped and turned, and found myself facing Levi of Kadesh, the handsome young soldier my husband was cheating.

CHAPTER
4

I bit my lip and said, "I did not know anyone listened." I felt my cheeks grow hot.

"How anyone could fail to listen to such sweet sounds is the real mystery," he said. "I would have thought every living creature here would have fallen in line behind you."

I laughed, knowing ridiculous flattery when I heard it. He smiled at me.

Oh, he smiled at me, and in the instant that he did, I wished that he had not. I had never known such yearning as I knew at that moment: that my parents had not given me in marriage to Heber, that I had not been from Hazor but instead from whichever hill town this man called home, that, like the dove, I could take to my wings and fly, fly, fly.

I took a step back from the well, feeling my mouth go dry, and said, "Please, you have a journey before you. Fill your water skins first."

His smile, if anything, grew sweeter. "Yours is the

33

first kindness I have had here since I arrived. Would that I were a king or a prince that all might treat me as the kings and princes must be treated here. And yet, if you would let me hear you laugh again, I would think myself luckier than any king."

The heat in my cheeks grew hotter, and I turned my face away from him and hid behind my hair, too embarrassed to look in his eyes any longer. I wore my red wool kuttonet, a parting gift from my mother, that draped over my left shoulder and left my right shoulder bare, and my head was uncovered. Gold bracelets jangled at my wrists and ankles. My manner of dress was no different from that of any other woman in the camp, yet when he looked at me, I felt like a temple dancer, or one of Ashtartu's sacred harlots.

"You blush, maiden," he said.

I shook my head, still hiding my face from him. "I am a wife of Heber," I told him. "The man who owes you a sword," I added, hoping that it would make him dislike me, so that he would turn and leave. A married woman dares not have the thoughts I had in those moments.

He was silent for so long, I thought he had done exactly that, and I turned to see if I might catch a glimpse of him walking away. He stood in exactly the same place he had stood before, still watching me, his head tipped to one side and a curling half-smile on his lips.

"I would not have thought to receive kindness from the house of Heber, O Heber's wife who has no name. But I thank you for it, and would ask to return it. Lower your water jar into the well, and when it's full, I will draw it up for you."

"You need not—you owe me no kindness. My husband was . . . I saw him . . . He treated you most ill."

"But you are not your husband, and your water jar will be quite heavy."

My sister-wives waited for me to return, and three more jars waited to be filled. I sighed and said, "Then I thank you," and took the knotted rope I carried with me, ran it through the handle, and lowered my kaddim into the well.

While it filled, he said, "And have you truly no name, little dove?"

"I am Jael," I told him.

"Jael, wife of Heber. I am Levi of Kadesh, and I thank you for giving this journey of mine one bright moment that I can hold in my heart on the long trip home."

"He'll have your sword finished for you next time," I blurted, and the words were no more past my lips than I wished to have them back.

Levi's eyebrows twitched. "Forgive me my unbelief," he said, "but I think he intends never to make my sword."

"He will," I said, my voice turning dogged and grim. "He is . . ." I faltered. I could not say of my husband that he was a good man, or that he was honorable in his dealings, or that I would talk to him and that he would listen to my counsel. He wasn't, and he wouldn't, and I could hardly say that Heber was the man I detested but that he was my husband and I would find a way to help this stranger in spite of who Heber was. "He will," I said again, and then looked down into the well. "The jar is full."

"This one jar seems not enough water to serve a household," Levi said as he lifted it out. I tried not to watch the muscles in his shoulders bunch as he lifted it quickly out of the well. I might as well have tried to fly like the dove. I could not turn my gaze from him.

"It isn't," I said. "I have four jars to . . ." And I faltered to a stop again. "To fill," I said.

He smiled and handed the jar to me. As I placed the rolled pad on my head and lifted the jar atop it, he said, "I'm glad we met, Jael, wife of Heber. And I hope you are right about the sword."

Relieved that he had not said he would help me with all four jars, I said, "I am sure he will." I did not say I was glad to have met him. I was, in fact, sure I would regret having met him, because it would take me a long time to chase him from my thoughts.

I walked away—and heard him humming the tune of my mother's dove and calf song.

"You took long enough," Talliya said when I returned. "Those gossiping children at the well never have any sense of all the work the rest of us have to do in a day."

I said, "I'll be quicker this time."

"I should hope so."

I had come to love Talliya, but until she had rinsed her face and hands and dressed for the day, she was no one to talk with.

I took the second jar with quicker steps, nodding to those I passed, but not stopping to talk, only saying, "Talliya is in a rush this morning." Everyone knew Talliya, and that she thrived on being demanding.

I did not see Levi when I reached the well, and I breathed a relieved sigh. I knotted the rope in the handle and lowered the kaddim into the well.

"How strange to meet you here," a voice right behind me said.

I jumped and nearly dropped my rope into the well. "If the rope drops, who will be the one who goes in to get it?" I asked him when my heart slowed in its wild beating.

"I would never let it drop," he said. "And I thought I might stay and help you with the rest of your water," he said.

I closed my eyes. "Do you imagine that my husband would be pleased that you stayed to help me?"

I heard him laugh, and looked over at him. "I'm sure he would not, and when I go I will go, and never bother you again. But you are such a sad little dove, for all your bright red feathers, and I am trying to

37

understand how a beautiful woman with a kind and loving husband could yet seem so terribly unhappy."

In my head, my mother's voice: *Ill words follow you home.*

That he was a man fair to look upon, I could not deny. That he was kind in his way, I could not deny. That he offered me an ear into which I might whisper my woes without the whole of the camp discovering my misery . . . Ah, what I would have given to have the right to whisper into that sympathetic ear.

But ill words follow you home. And should I have dared to speak, and mine followed me back to Heber's ears, I could fear worse than a beating.

So I said nothing.

He reached past me when the kaddim filled, and pulled my water from the well. His smile was sad as he handed the jar to me and watched me balance it on my head.

"I wish I had met you sooner," he said. "I wish I had known your parents, that I could have . . . ." His voice died away, and he shrugged. "No matter. Why give the wind the secrets of the heart? The wind never keeps secrets." He stepped out of my way. "I wish you well, sad little dove. I wish you love, and many children, and joy to the end of your days."

"As I wish for you," I said around a lump that formed in my throat. I blinked back tears, and hoped that he did not see me do so.

I would not have love. I would not have children

unless I made myself an adulteress to do so. I would not have joy—to the end of my days, or ever.

My parents had done the best for me that they could—or thought they had. They had known only the rich and charming man who had offered well for their daughter and who had said the right things. They had not known the Heber who ruled within his tent. They had never seen the man who had chosen a young, wide-hipped girl to take the childbearing place of his older wife and concubine, to provide him with sons and workers into his old age.

They had never met Heber the drinker. Heber the dried stalk.

I walked away from the well, fighting back tears. Heber was not their fault. And he was not mine. I could not change him, I could not fix him, and I could not leave him, so I had to make the best of my situation. I had to find joy in the parts of each day that were not my husband.

I had my sister-wives for friendship. Talliya's babies for children. A good home, the comfort of daily chores, the knowledge that I had a place.

I would not think of the young soldier with the kind smile again, I promised myself. It was not my place to think of how things might have been. It was my place to find satisfaction in each day.

I swung the second jar down on the floor and lifted up the third, not saying anything when I did, because I was in a hurry to return to the well.

I could see his eyes. His smile. His strong hands offering me the kaddim full of water.

I would not think of him ever again, after I helped him get his sword back. I made myself that promise, and thought of what I might tell him when I returned to the well.

But when I got there, he was gone.

Gone. And like as not, I would not see him again. I would be elsewhere when he came for his sword, elsewhere when he and Heber argued, and in a while, he would seem like a dream to me.

He did not seem like a dream that day, though. I was so near useless, Pigat asked me if I was sick, and I lied and told her my head ached as if with fever, and she made me lie down for a while until I was better.

And while I lay there, I thought about how I might help Levi of Kadesh receive the sword my husband owed him.

CHAPTER
5

The lot of us were spinning while we tended the children, talking and laughing. Pigat spun wool, Talliya spun goats' hair, and I—with a new, differently balanced spindle and distaff—worked with flax, which was the easiest fiber to make into thread.

"At the well just yesterday, I heard that Atiya the goatherd's wife is with child," I said, and Pigat said, "Atiya, if she keeps to her practice of bringing forth girls, will provide wives for every man's son in this camp."

"She seems determined to try," Talliya said softly. "Would that I would have a daughter, to walk with me and spin with me and give me granddaughters when I am old."

"Sons are more of a blessing," Pigat said.

But no longer were we laughing, and I wished I had not mentioned the fertile Atiya and her many, many daughters.

We spun in silence for a little while, lost in our

own thoughts, until from Heber's side of the tent, we heard our husband enter. And with him was the booming voice of another man—a voice I did not know.

"Welcome to my humble abode, dear friend," Heber said. "All that is mine is yours. Take your rest within my tent—tarry awhile, and I will bring water to wash your feet, and give you a bit of bread that you will not go hungry."

"You are most kind, beloved brother," said the stranger, and I saw loathing in Pigat's eyes. "I can stay only a little while; my men and I are so eager to return to Hazor and give our gifts and our good news to our families that we travel even at night, like jackals."

"Like jackals, indeed." Pigat still wore fury on her face. "That's Sisera, Jabin's general," she whispered to me. "He's foul, vile—brother of a jackal, brother of a vulture."

"Worse than our husband?" I whispered back.

"A thousand times worse."

This I had to see with my own eyes. When Heber called "Wife!" it was I who put aside my spinning and went through to his side of the tent to greet him and his guest.

"What would you have, my husband?" I asked.

"Lehem and nazid, Wife, halab and yayin and hem'a. Bring them quickly—you stand before the great general Sisera, the bravest man in Canaan, Jabin's hero, my friend and brother."

I ducked my head in greeting. "My lord," I said, and hurried quickly away. Sisera might be no brother of blood, but he was in truth a brother in spirit. He was another like Heber—fat and red-faced, loud and bold and staring, with a disagreeable smile and a mouth cruel as a whetted blade.

He sat in the place of honor, with Heber at his side grinning like a dog with a fresh bone, and with Heber's older sons arrayed around him, taking their share of glory from their proximity to the great man.

I wished then that I had not let my curiosity get the better of me, that I had not leapt to be first to answer our husband's command. Just looking at Sisera, I felt fear slip into my blood like a winter chill.

"You've a fine new mare in your stable," Sisera said as I scurried through to the women's side of the tent. "You may have no use for the gift I've brought back from battle for you."

"That one looks comely enough," Heber said, and sighed. "But the gods have never set foot upon this earth a more tiresome, foolish child. Were she not a good worker, I'd have divorced her and sent her back to her parents; I'd rather have another temple whore any day."

I felt the fire burn in my cheeks, and saw that my sister-wife and Talliya looked upon me with pity.

43

"Then you might find joy in my little war trophy after all," Sisera boomed. "I've brought a concubine for you, fresh from her parents' house, pure as spring water, and young enough to give you many a strong-backed boy." He clapped his hands once, sharply, and I heard movement on the other side of the tent. "And such a man you are, Heber my brother, to sire only sons," the general added.

The three of us exchanged glances. No one laughed; we had nothing we dared laugh about. If Heber could have fathered anything at all, Pigat and Talliya would not have been adulteresses, nor I faced with a future of childlessness or adultery.

All spinning was put aside as we gathered food. The nazim that day, a stew of red peppers and lentils, almonds and fresh vegetables and herbs, had been cooking slowly in the sir, the wide-mouthed cook pot, for the better part of the day. As the sun dropped toward the horizon, the spicy scent of it already filled our tent. The lehem, flat bread, Pigat had made just after sunrise. It waited in its basket, wrapped in clean cloths. The halab, curdled goat's milk, I had made that morning, first milking the goats and then rocking the leather skin no'd in which we stored the milk to form the curdles. The cream Talliya had taken and churned to butter, and then boiled to the refined, clear oil called hem'a. And yayin, the wine of grapes, we had in plenty, for did not Heber love to rock himself to sleep in its embrace?

Were there not a guest, all of us, Heber and wives, concubines and sons, would have eaten together from the pot, sopping the stew with our bread. But because of Heber's guest, the first meal would be for the men only, and would be served as a feast, even if we had no lamb to slaughter, or time to prepare it. Sisera's surprise visit left us ill prepared.

My sister-wives and I carried out the baskets and pots and drinking bowls for Heber and Sisera and all the older sons, piled high with food. Neither we nor the two little boys would eat until the men had finished, and we would make do with what remained, or if too little remained, we would prepare a quick meal for ourselves of parched grain and bread dipped in wine or olive oil and salt. Sisera looked to me to be a man of many appetites, none of them modest. I did not anticipate tasting the fine stew that had been perfuming the tent for most of the day.

The girl he had brought was a pretty creature, younger than I by a year or so, with her wrists bound before her and her pale blue dress rent and soiled. She looked like she had put up a fight, I thought. Not that it had done her any good.

"Take that one with you," Haber said to us. "And bathe her, and dress her in something acceptable. And bring her to me tonight."

The girl's head came up with a snap, and I saw anguish and fire in her eyes. "It is the way of my people, and the law of my God, that as I was taken captive from my home, I shall have a month to cut my hair and pare my nails and mourn the family that I shall never see again."

Heber laughed. "Which god's foolish rule is that, little slave? For I assure you, not El or Asherah, nor Baal or Anat, nor Ashtartu has such a law."

"My God is Yahweh-Shalom," she said. "The One God."

"Not anymore," Heber told her. "Your gods are my gods, and your laws are as I set them out for you, and no other way. You'll go into the women's tent, and you'll bathe and make yourself presentable, and tonight you will bring yourself unto me, and you will please me."

We took her away quickly, Pigat and Talliya and I, because we could see the storm brewing in her eyes, and it would not do for her to argue with Heber in front of a man of such importance as Sisera. Heber would kill her for that, and in doing so would probably insult Sisera for so treating his gift.

In the women's side of the tent, the girl turned to us and said, "But it is the *law*. God's *law* that women taken as captive are not to be given away to others, but if their captor does not want them, then they are to be set free and returned to their people. That fiend Sisera did not want me for himself or for his sons, but he would not let me go, either. I have been given to this . . . this . . . man against Yahweh's law, and this idolator tells me that I cannot worship Yahweh-Shalom, and I cannot mourn the loss of my family, but that he will have me serve him tonight?''

I told her, ''We cannot help you with your god's rules and laws. And you will have to go in to him tonight. But as for worshipping your god, you can do that easily enough.'' I pointed to our row of house gods sitting in their pottery shrines. ''Put up a shrine to him, and make your offerings to him when you offer to the other gods. None of us will complain about another god, so long as he is not another blood-drinking god.''

''We could hide this Yahweh-Shalom's idol,'' Pigat said, ''if he is the sort of god that would anger Heber. He doesn't require wine as a sacrifice, does he? Grain we have in plenty, and wool, water, salt, and fat. But our wine Heber watches like a widow watches her portion, and as for babies—well, Heber has already fed one child to the fires of Baal, and will not willingly sacrifice another.''

The girl shook her head. ''Yahweh-Shalom is the One God, the True God. He is not a little god of stone, and He forbids the sacrifice of children or of any humans. He is spirit, all around us and in us, uplifting us. All other gods are false gods that lead away from Him.''

She turned from us, and Pigat and Talliya and I

looked at each other. This girl was clearly going to be trouble for us. If she took her speech about her One God to Heber, Heber would almost certainly throw her into the square and have her stoned, or dedicate her to Ashtartu to be a temple whore. He had given his firstborn son to Baal, and to hear some girl tell him that Baal was no god at all. . . .

No. He would not take gently to her words.

I knew Heber's fists. I did not want to see this new girl suffer under them. I started to go to her, but Pigat shook her head and beckoned me over.

"You think you can talk sense into her?"

"I can try," I said.

"She's not going to listen to you. She has her One God, and until Heber has beaten her One God out of her, she is going to be impossible. I've seen these people before, Jael. They are stubborn even unto death."

"But what if she says to our husband what she said to us, and he kills her?" I whispered.

Pigat looked at me with sad, knowing eyes. "What if he does? You're young, Jael. You haven't yet discovered that there are some people who cannot be helped. By the look of things, she is one of those."

But I watched her standing with her back to us, her wrists still bound, with her torn dress and the dirt on her clothes and body testifying to how hard she had fought for her freedom, and my heart went out to her. She was someplace she did not want to be. So was I. She was to be given to a man who would hurt her and shame her, just as I had been.

I kept thinking there must be something I could do for her to help her. To save her from herself.

I took one of our work knives and went over to her. "Have you a name?"

"Achaia," she told me warily. "It means 'sorrowing,' or 'sad.' "

I wondered if the gods would have looked on her more favorably if her parents had named her something that meant "happy." Or "fortunate."

"I'm Jael. Give me your wrists," I said. "I'll cut your bindings."

Her skin beneath the thick knots of cloth was raw, and I could see when I looked closer that she had tried to work the knots free with her teeth. Half of what I'd taken for dirt was actually bruised skin. She seemed to me a wild thing; she glared through her tangled hair with fierce eyes, and I could see her as a lioness on the hunt. She was unlike me in that regard—she was neither meek nor obedient.

I envied her ferocity. Had I such courage, I might have found a way to run back to my parents house to hide. Or found some other way to freedom.

But I was not a brave woman. I would never be, I thought; such was not my nature.

I pointed out Pigat and Talliya, and named them for her so that she would know them.

"Listen," I told her, "our husband shouts and hits.

49

He drinks wine, and the wine sets free a cruel spirit in him. You must not anger him with your talk of your god or your laws. He owns you now, as he owns all of us, and our lot is cast together, yours and ours. So long as we are quiet and obedient, we have food sufficient to our needs and a place to sleep. So long as we please him and bear him sons, he does not beat us much. But if you speak to him as you have spoken to us . . . Little Sister, he will kill you this very night."

"It would be better to be dead than to be here," she said, and I saw that her eyes had filled with tears.

"No," I told her. "It would *not.*" And then I told her what I told myself each night that Heber called for me instead of Talliya, in the moments before I pushed through the flap to the other side of the tent. "If you are alive, all the world can change in a day. There is always hope for something better." I thought of Levi of Kadesh, who had been one of her people. How kind he had been. How gentle he would be. It was not my place to hope, yet I could imagine myself taken as captive by the Israelites, to be Levi's concubine, stolen away from my rightful husband as this girl had been stolen away from her home. I could imagine how things might one day be better, even if I had to become a slave for them to be so.

Yes. All the world could change in a day.

But it would not change this day. "But this is your home now, no matter how much you or I would wish otherwise. Do as Heber tells you, make yourself clean and presentable, let us anoint your hair with oil and perfume. Maybe for you it will not go as badly as it went for me."

It would, of course. I suspected that Heber lacked whatever a man needed to make things go well. Sympathy. Empathy.

Humanity?

CHAPTER
6

The next morning, Achaia rejoined us. We barely dared to look at her; the sounds from the other side of the tent the night before had been so bad, the littlest boys had awakened, crying with fear.

Achaia wore both the green kuttonet we had dressed her in the night before, and over that, a simla, a cloak in which she wrapped herself so only her fingertips showed. She had veiled her face with a heavy sa'ip, so that we could see nothing but her eyes—but of them we could see enough to imagine the rest.

Pigat set up the bathing corner so that Achaia could have some privacy, and I brought water.

He had done everything he could to hurt her without permanently breaking her. I had thought he'd used me badly, but I had not imagined the sort of viciousness of which he was capable.

My dislike for my husband turned to hatred in that moment. My sister-wives were as quiet as I, as shocked

52

to speechlessness. We helped her get herself clean, we helped her put on clothes, and we winced with her for each movement she took.

Talliya brought forth her cosmetics, and out of it offered the black kohl and the rich green malachite with which she did her own eyes, and with long, graceful fingers, she painted Achaia's eyes to hide the bruises Heber had left even there. Then we wrapped her again in her kuttonet and lay her on a mat away from the children, and we covered her with her simla. Another day she would help us with the cooking and the child-watching, the spinning and the weaving and the dyeing. But that day, not one of us could bear to think of her doing anything at all.

When she was asleep, Pigat and Tallia and I began the day's work, grinding grain, chopping peppers, slicing olives and almonds, cleaning the lentils and the beans. We kept our voices low as we talked. Pigat sent the older children out to gather straw and twigs for our fire, and once they were gone, she turned to me.

"Near two months have you been with us now," she said, "and you have not yet visited with Keret or made your special offering to Baal. Heber has been patient, but his patience will not last. It is for children that he brought you into this house, Jael, for my days of childbearing are past, and Talliya has had her last child, as well, though Heber does not yet know it. He will have to try himself on her awhile longer before he becomes convinced. It is your duty to give him sons."

I had known this talk would be coming. To keep peace in the household, I would have to have children, for Heber's work depended upon strong young sons to keep the business growing. Sisera had nine hundred ironclad chariots, I was told, and the Kenite camp had only a few families of smiths skilled in the working of forged iron. Heber and his sons were special; they stood above the men who worked only in bronze and copper and silver and gold.

But I could not reconcile what I had to do with what I feared to do. I lived in dread of being found out, not just for myself but for Pigat and Talliya, as well. My death would like as not be their deaths.

"I will do as I must," I told them, "but not yet. I pray each day at Baal's shrine that he will honor Heber and me with children, as the oracle promised. I do not want to be guilty of rushing a god, and—" I took a deep breath"—perhaps Heber's stalk will bear fruit eventually."

Neither Talliya nor Pigat could argue with that. The miracles of the gods were beyond human understanding. But the ears of the gods seemed to me beyond human reach, too, and I held out little hope for a miracle. I had prayed that Heber would be a good husband, and the auguries had portended great happiness and fertility for the two of us.

But neither the gods nor Heber had delivered. The

oracle had been wrong, completely wrong, totally wrong, and I found myself wondering if the fault of that lay with the oracle, or with the gods themselves.

I did not know.

When the bread was done and the stew was cooking, we returned to spinning. Canaanites are master weavers and master dyers—of all the civilized world, we alone know the secret of the rich purple dye we make from the seaside snails. But the snails are hard to come by, and the vinegar and other ingredients we use to bring out the color are tricky to work with in the right combinations. The thread we spun would be dyed in the deep blue that comes from the indigo plants to the lands south of us. Heber had just traded for a good lot of the indigo, along with sheep's wool and flax, in exchange for working metal for the trading caravan that came through. Once we had the whole lot spun and dyed and woven, Heber, his sons, his wives, and his concubines would be radiant in new robes and have cloth left over to trade, perhaps.

My one hand drew flax from the distaff, feeding it to my other hand, from which hung my light spindle. With the weight of the spindle whorl keeping it going, I drafted the fibers between my fingers, letting the twist work itself into the thread. The movements of spinning I had learned as a child at my mother's knee, first making fat yarns that were all lumps and bumps, and then learning to draw the thread out to a great fineness. My mother let me work with all the wonderful fibers she obtained. Of them, I liked flax least. But then, I was the youngest of the women in this household, and so found myself making flax again, as if I were a child. We would appreciate the lighter material in hot weather, but I wished Pigat and Talliya had borne daughters as well as sons, so that the children could be turned to the flax.

To some extent, though, spinning is spinning.

The spindle that winds the threads unwinds the thoughts, as we always say. And it unwound my knotted thoughts about how Heber might be tricked into giving Levi of Kadesh the sword he had promised. How he might, in other words, be led into doing the right thing rather than the wrong one.

I kept my eyes on that middle distance between my work and the two boys, where I could watch both while seeing neither, and said, "Do you recall the man from Kadesh whose sword Heber did not have finished the last time he came here?"

"Or the time before that, or the time even before that. I recall him well enough," Pigat said.

"I heard at the well this morning that the young man is not just a common soldier, but is in fact a prince, and that he dressed as a common soldier to find out how his men would be treated if they brought their business to Heber."

Both Pigat and Talliya put their spindles in their bowls and tucked their distaffs into their hagoras, the long sashes wound several times around their waists. "You are sure of this?" Pigat said.

"For Heber has much work to keep him paid now, but in slow times, a new prince with soldiers to arm would be a great boon," Talliya said.

I turned to Talliya first. "It would, but we are unlikely enough to see such a boon." And then to Pigat, I said, "Of course I am not sure. This was a thing I heard at the well, and you know how unreliable such chatterings are. Still, I thought this tale worth the mention, since it concerns our household. I heard that this young prince said in anger to one of his men that he would return but once more, and that already he was certain that Heber should have none of his business, and perhaps none of the Kenites at this camp would."

And I turned my face back to my work, and kept any hint of smile from my lips.

Pigat and Talliya fell into a deep conference, in which they ignored me entirely. "That could be a disaster," Talliya said. "The word of a common soldier does not carry much weight, but the word of a prince, murmured into the right ears, that Heber is unreliable could slow his business to a trickle."

"Heber has Jabin and Sisera and the whole of the army of Canaan to draw on. The word of a enemy prince, though prince he might be, will have no weight with them."

"But kings are fickle. Remember how Sisera drew

business away from Velabaal and his sons when Velabaal's ironwork turned out to be less well forged than Heber's. Remember how for so long Velabaal called Sisera his brother and friend, and how when Sisera stopped visiting Velabaal's tent, so did most of his other customers. No one wanted his work anymore. The family has been reduced to doing bangles and rings for women."

"They aren't starving," Pigat said, clearly not wanting to have to consider the consequences of Heber being Heber.

"But still, Heber has the choice work. And the best fees, and the most customers. You know other smiths are envious of his popularity. If they get hold of something like this, they'll use it against him, to get his business for themselves."

"They will," Pigat said, nodding and frowning.

Talliya picked up her spindle again. "But what can we do?"

"We dare not spread the word any further, or let it get back to him from anyone other than us," Pigat said.

"I cannot tell him," Talliya said. "And Jael cannot."

"No. Nor can the sleeping child over there." She sighed. "But I can tell him. Before we take his wine in to him tonight, I will go to him and tell him what I have heard, and what I have found, and what I believe he must do to undo any damage his thought-lessness has caused.''

I felt content inside. I had done something good, something that would hurt no one, that would help both Levi and Heber, and would let me fulfill the promise I had given to the stranger. I would be able to let my conscience rest. Would be able to forget about Levi of Kadesh now, and keep my mind in my own household, and on my own husband. I could attend to my prayers and hope for my miracle.

I looked over at the still-sleeping Achaia, and wondered what sort of prayers she prayed, and what sort of miracle she asked her strange One God to deliver to her.

CHAPTER
7

"It's a simple thing," I told Achaia. "You kneel before each shrine, and give the offering preferred by that god. And then you pray, asking each god by name for that which you would have. Ask only for little things—the priests alone pray for prosperity, and weather, and victory over our enemies."

Achaia, still bruised days later, had not been back to Heber's quarters. After their first night together, he had not called for her again. Neither he nor she had said a word of why. As unsatisfactory as he had found me, I could tell that he was much more displeased with her.

Achaia seemed happy enough with that. And she was still completely unwilling to fit herself into our household. She had strict rules about how she would drink milk or eat meat, about how foods had to be prepared, about which foods could be prepared together.

But we discovered to our great delight that she loved cooking, and was entirely willing to take over everything but basic grain preparation. She was very capable of figuring quantities of food for the number of mouths we fed each night, and everything she made was delicious. So with gratitude we had passed cooking over to her, though Pigat refused to give up her bread-making. Good bread is an art, and among the Kenites, Pigat was reckoned an artist. What sort of woman would Pigat be if she placed her art in the hands of an outsider and a concubine who did not know the finer points of Pigat's oven or Pigat's secret recipes?

So while Achaia diced olives and I spun, we talked in low voices.

"I will not worship your idols. My God does not permit it."

"Your God is going to see you dead. I don't see him sending rescuers for you," I told her.

"Yahweh-Shalom tests those he loves."

"All priests say the same thing. Those the gods love are tested. Except when they say that those the gods love are rewarded. Either way, it turns out the priests are always right: Whether you are rich as kings or starving in an alley, you're doing so because the gods have decided that is what you should be doing."

"Have you ever seen a miracle?" Achaia asked me,

interrupting my complaints against the gods, who were not sending anyone rushing to my rescue, either.

"No. I have heard tell of them, but always from the selfsame priests who would have my pain be proof the gods love me."

"I saw a miracle once."

This interested me.

"In our town, there had been neither water nor food for three days, and we knew that we would starve. Our cisterns were empty, and the Canaanite armies had surrounded our town and had blocked off all food coming to us. Any of our people who tried to step out into the fields to work, they killed. So we had nothing."

"That's terrible."

"Not as terrible as what they did two years later, but that had nothing to do with my miracle."

"Tell me about your miracle, then."

"The priests called all of us together. It was summer, and the sky had no clouds in it. We would have no rain for another month—we all knew this, and knew as well that we would be dead when at last the rains did fall, and that they would do nothing for us but bury what remained of our carcasses in mud."

I nodded.

"But the priests told us to lift up our eyes to the heavens, and ask of Yahweh-Shalom that He have mercy on us."

I waited, watching the smile that spread slowly across her face.

"The priests said Yahweh-shalom had told them to take the covers off the cisterns at dawn, which you know we never do in the summer."

"Of course not. The sun dries all the water."

"And yet, with all of us outside praying, and with the priests drawing covers off the cisterns in the temple and the men taking the covers off the cisterns around the rest of the town, the sun rose. And as the last cover came off, a mighty, twisting wind came up, and out of the cloudless sky fell a rain as hard as a winter rain. But it was not just a rain. In with the pouring water were living fishes, and when they fell on the ground, we picked them up. And when they fell into the cisterns, they lived, so that we had water to drink and fish to eat. Fortified by our God, our men went out by night and hamstrung the horses of the enemy, and rained down arrows upon the men, until the encamped Canaanites fled, and did not return to our town for two years."

In fact, I remembered something about that incident. Something about a rain of fishes that fed a hilltop town. The Canaanites were my people. The Canaanite gods were my gods. But the God of Israel sounded like a better God, one who might be supplicated in a time of trouble, and who might offer real help in need.

Fishes from the sky. I had thought the tale a fanciful one told by men who had been beaten by an inferior enemy.

I didn't need a miracle of fishes and rain from a cloudless sky. I needed something smaller. Something simpler. I needed only for my husband to have a change of heart and for his seed to take in my womb—or, if I could not have those things, then I needed a way out of this situation that a timid young woman taught from birth to be obedient might dare to take.

One that did not involve adultery.

"If this god of yours will not permit you to keep a shrine with his idol in it, if you may not say his name, how are you to ask him for his help? If you need the priests to offer up prayers for you, how will he hear you here?"

Achaia carefully sliced almonds, and I let the thread run through my fingers. "He hears the words of our hearts," she said. "He hears the thoughts of our minds. He sees our deeds, and he feels our suffering. Whenever we turn our faces toward him, he has already seen what we need, and already knows what we will ask."

"If your god knows what you need before you tell him, why must you ever pray at all?"

"It is part of our berit, our covenant with Yahweh-Shalom, that he will be our God, and we will be His people. It is not enough that Yahweh-Shalom see our need and answer it. We must also see our need and ask that He meet it, and when He has met it, we must give thanks. Otherwise we will not know He is present in our lives, and we will fall away from Him.'' She scraped the almonds into the sir, and sighed. "Some fall away anyway, for it is easier to complain than to act, and easier to be ungrateful than to give thanks.''

I considered what she said. I considered the price I would pay, should Heber discover that I, his true wife, had followed his out-of-favor concubine Achaia into the worship of her god, while turning away from Heber's gods and the gods of my own family.

But I considered, as well, that Baal had not yet granted me a child. And if Pigat and Talliya were right, he never would, no matter what the oracle had foretold on my wedding day.

I considered that Baal had not made Heber into a kind or a gentle man.

I considered that I had not much courage. But I had a little. Perhaps enough to worship Achaia's god and hide the truth.

But perhaps not.

"Are you certain that you would not like me to teach you the prayers to Asherah, and to Anat, and to Ashtartu? They are a woman's gods. They are like us—mother, maiden, and whore.''

"No,'' Achaia told me. "Yahweh-Shalom lives inside me, and blesses me daily with His love and gifts. I would have to be someone else to turn away from Him."

I could not see where her god had given her many blessings. He had allowed Achaia to be taken from her people, given to Heber in a home where she was not permitted to worship Him, and beaten until her skin looked like bruised fruit.

I asked her about this.

"Yahweh-Shalom has his reasons. Always. If I am here, it is for a reason. So I will make myself useful, and I will pray daily, and I will wait for His words on my heart, that I might know why I am here."

She went back to cooking, and I returned my attention to my spinning, and to keeping an eye on the little boys as they played within the tent, and to thinking.

It was interesting to consider that a god might have a purpose for a woman's life. A purpose for *my* life other than the one my husband decreed. To my husband, my purpose was to do my work within the household and bear him children.

If I began to pray to Achaia's god, would He have a purpose for me?

CHAPTER
8

The Kenite encampment did not have its own market.

I had been accustomed, with my mother and father and sister and brothers, to visit the market in Hazor, which held within it all the wonders of the world, brought to our city by ships and then caravans from the far reaches of the world. Lamps we found there of curious make, and sandals of both our own fashion and the fashion of foreigners; honey and olive oil; jewelry and glass of many colors; combs for our hair and fine cloth for robes; jewelry of every imaginable sort; fruits both dried and fresh, seeds and grains, nuts and berries. Wool dyed and undyed, spun and unspun we found; wool unboiled and still rich with lanolin as if just sheared from the sheep; and goat hair uncarded and unspun; and long-fibered flax to spin into the finest linen.

I'd loved the market with its barterers and banterers, its narrow paths and close-pressing crowds, its air hanging smoky and rich with the scents of cooking food to buy and take away, its laughter and shouting.

The Kenite camp had no market. But on rare mornings, caravans would arrive and set up stalls outside the camp.

While it was still dark I woke to hear Latiya the wife of Zimriqart, Pigat's eldest son, hissing at us with her head poked through our tent flap like a wayward camel. "Up, quick, and dress, for the market has come in the night, and will open its stalls at daybreak.

We splashed our faces with water from a kad, all four of us. Achaia and I were quicker about it. Young bones and strong backs we had, and a deep desire to see something bright and new and exciting.

But neither Pigat nor Talliya was far behind us. We would have the credit of Heber's name and his wealth behind us when we shopped; we would go and buy for the household, but also for ourselves, and present to him our purchases, and Heber would pay.

It was as a festival day, with households hurrying toward the traders and their stalls to see what wonders might be hidden within the crowded rows.

And, ah, the scent. Already the air was fragrant with incense and cooking grains and fruits. Up close, though, some among this group of traders had a gaunt and sickly look about them. I did not like their coughing and sneezing, or the bright glassiness in their eyes, or the pallor of their lips and fingertips. I pointed them out to Achaia, and we agreed to avoid those stalls.

Achaia spotted something in one stall full of glittering baubles, however, and grabbed my hand and pulled me forward. We ran, laughing like children, and crowded up against the edge of the wagon, beneath the awning, as close as we could get to the pretty things. A merchant had brought beads of bone and glass, silver and polished stone, some strung, and some unstrung. I could imagine the fine jewelry we could make with them. One little glass face of Asherah I found too precious to pass by, and asked the merchant to set it aside for me. Achaia, meanwhile, found a complete string of blue beads, half of glass and half of polished stone. I thought them as lovely as she did, and when she held them to her throat, I could see how fine they would look, so we added them to Heber's tally, and the merchant set them aside for us, as well, marked with his seal and Heber's name.

We did not waste time at the woven goods. We were both skilled weavers and would rather do our own fabrics, which were as fine as any we saw. I could dye, too, but some unspun wool rovings, already dyed, lay in piles on one trader's cart. This time I pulled Achaia forward. There was a blue there that I had never seen before. It was a gemstone blue,

and not a color I would have been able to make with
indigo. Indigo and something else, perhaps, but I
could not imagine what. The gloss and crimp of the
wool I could imagine running through my fingers as
I spun, and when I put my face to it, it smelled clean
and still full of lanolin, which would shed the winter
rains. A cloak, I thought. Or a kuttonet. For me.

"Blue is a sacred color to Yahweh-Shalom," Achaia
said. "Blue is the color of the sky, the place where
our hand reaches up and His reaches down. It is the
color of our covenant with Him."

"So I should not buy this?" I asked. "It would be
an offense to your god if I bought it? Or wore it?"

"That isn't what I meant at all." Her smile was
enigmatic. "It is beautiful. You should buy it. When
you wear it, you'll think of the sky. . . ."

I did buy it, the whole lot, with which I would
spin for myself fine blue thread, and a lovely blue
kuttonet.

We wandered on. Pigat as first wife was responsible for making sure we had all the necessities—she
knew from long practice how much grain to lay in
and how much dried fruit would last until the next
likely visit. Still, there were ways Achaia and I could
make ourselves useful, and we did. Mostly, though,
we played the part of children, *ooh*ing and *ahh*ing
over fine sandals of dyed dolphin leather and ankle
bracelets with tiny bronze bells.

And, "Oh, look, Jael," Achaia said, and pulled me

again toward something she saw. It was a little pottery stand, and the style of the pots and jugs were unfamiliar to me. They were without decoration, but beautifully made.

One in particular she pointed out to me, a baqbuq, which is a carafe for pouring wine. "My father made pottery," she told me. "That looks so much like his work. Always he signed his pots with a little falcon on the bottom, for his name meant 'falcon.' "

She turned the pot over to show me where he signed them. And on the bottom was a little falcon, etched into the clay with a scribe.

Her eyes filled with tears. "He is dead now, my father. I saw him die. That monster Sisera killed him, when my father would have kept the Canaanite army from pillaging our house and stealing me and my sisters away."

I pointed out the pot up to the trader and said, "We must have this pot, please."

How could Achaia not have it? Heber might see no purpose in it, for we already had a carafe. Perhaps we had no need for another, but this was something from her father's hands, something precious, something that she could never find again if we let this opportunity pass.

The trader marked it for us, and we passed on. We bought lamp oil—a task with which Pigat had charged us—and a new lamp to replace one Talliya's toddler in his tumbling had managed to break.

All too soon the traders were packing up their stalls, and our husband was reckoning his bill with them.

Heber looked over the pile of items we had selected, and did not raise his voice a single time. He did not seem even to notice the few little trinkets we had obtained for ourselves, or the extra carafe which would sit with our other pottery.

He had made good friends with the wine merchant, I saw, and had laid in another supply of wine from vineyards near the sea.

I could not help but think that we borrowed his good mood now for the foul temper he would be sure to display later.

But it mattered not. The beads we would hide away, the baqbuq put into use, and the wool we would make into such fine things that he would have no cause to accuse us of being wasteful.

Back in our tent, with much of the work of the day left undone, we set about unpacking and dividing up and storing our day's haul, and then Achaia and I got to work on the evening meal. We had early vegetables and interesting fruits and grains from far away, and we put them together into a honeyed grain dish, with sliced raw fruit and vegetables so highly spiced, they made my eyes water and my tongue hang out. "We'll need all the bread Pigat can make to survive that," I said as Achaia laughed at me.

From out by her tannur where she crouched, alternating between tossing the raw dough into the beehive-shaped oven's hot interior and fishing out the finished bread with her matteh-lehem—her bread stick—Pigat grinned at me. "She gives me a challenge?"

"All of us, I think," I told her. "Achaia wants to see if our tongues will blister with her sauce, but I think your bread will save us."

We laughed. It was a happy moment.

We sat together that night, Heber and his grown-but-unmarried son from Pigat, and his still beardless son from Talliya, and Pigat and Talliya and her two little boys, and Achaia and me, dipping our bread into the vegetables and sauce and wondering at the peppers that had made it such a fury. We enjoyed the honeyed grain, we relaxed, Heber and his sons sang a song; then we four women sang another.

That moment was what I hoped for. If Baal could just keep things as they were, I would not need to consider Achaia and her lonely One God.

But such happiness was not to be.

CHAPTER
9

Two nights later, Pigat woke from night terrors with a fever. Her mouth was dry, her skin hot to the touch, and she kept becoming confused. Others in the camp had starting showing signs of the same sickness the day before. Talliya said it had come with the traders, though Mot's priest said Mot sought a harvest of flesh.

We cooled Pigat's skin with water, and gave her water to drink as long as she would take it. I knew of herbs that sometimes helped, as did Talliya; we prepared them for her in a strong tea, and she sipped as she could, but as the night wore on, the fever burned hotter in her. Heber, to my surprise, came when I sought him, and when he saw the state of her, first brought in the priests to pray over her and sacrifice for her, and when he had done that, carried the water jars and brought back water from the well. I would never have thought him willing to do such a thing.

But he crouched beside her, holding her hand, talking to her about when the two of them were young. It was then that I discovered, for the first time, that once she had been the wife of his heart. That he had chosen her when the two of them were young together. He had loved her. And to my surprise, it seemed he still did.

As Pigat grew sicker, Heber promised her that he would put the rest of us away if only she would live for him. That he was sorry he had sought another wife against her counsel. That he would give her anything she desired, if she would just stay with him and not leave him alone.

She labored with her breathing, her stomach rising as her chest fell, her chest rising as her stomach fell. When she coughed, we had to turn her to her side so that she did not drown in the thick fluids that filled her lungs. The sounds she made were terrible; her suffering was terrible.

But with the dawn, Pigat's mind cleared, and she seemed to struggle less to draw breath. Her fever was still with her, but the priest declared that he had done his work, and that she would be well. He left to fill the air with smoke in some other tent.

Pigat waited until he was gone, then sat up. She was terribly weak, and her eyes glittered with a frightening shine. She licked dry lips, but when we tried to give her water, she pushed it away.

"I see fire," Pigat said to Heber. "I see fire, and

darkness in the sky, Husband of my youth, and a doom that creeps toward you. A shadow has come upon you. You feed it. You feed your doom." Her hand whipped out and grabbed on to his arm; she seemed to all of us at that moment an apparition, a seer peering from our world into the next. "Send it away. Hurry."

Heber's lips went gray, and a thin sheen of sweat glazed his forehead. "How, Wife of my youth? How do I send it away?"

"Be just. Be truthful. Be honorable." She fell back on the mat, and all the tension that had animated her washed out of her. "Be kind."

She turned her head away from all of us who gathered around her, and drew another breath, slowly, but this was a shallow breath. And when she let it out, she did not draw another.

We waited, and then Heber turned away from us, and for the first and last time, I saw him weep.

Talliya tore her hair and wailed, and tore at her clothes. I, too, cried out in mourning, as did Achaia, who had come to love kindly Pigat.

Heber's older sons entered, and they saw what had become of her; her own son dropped to his knees beside her and begged her wake. Talliya's older boy ran out of the tent, and we heard him spreading the word to his married brothers and half brothers in their own tents.

A crowd gathered, but the men who were her sons

and brothers stayed with her husband in the men's side of the tent. Meanwhile, Achaia and Talliya and I, as well as Pigat's friends, washed her and dressed her in her finest wheat-gold kuttonet, and around her neck we put necklaces of beads and carved shells, and around her ankles and wrists, bracelets and bells. I brushed her hair and in it put her two favorite combs, both of them carved with almond blossoms. Talliya painted her eyes with kohl and malachite. Achaia wrapped Pigat's purple hagora around her waist. It was the costliest thing that Pigat had owned; she had embroidered the finely woven wool with flowers of a paler purple, and with red and yellow, until it looked like a meadow in springtime.

She lay on the bier, and when we had wept over her and said our prayers for her, each in our own way, we stepped aside. The priests came and anointed her with myrrh, and they lifted her up, with her husband and her sons and brothers alongside her. We women fell behind, weeping and tearing our hair and clothes, and walked to the pyre that the rest of the men of the camp had built.

Heber kissed Pigat's cheek, and his tears fell on her; then at the priests' word, he stepped back, and the priests put her on the pyre—and with her, two slaughtered lambs and two doves. They prayed to Mot, the God of Death, Father of the Underworld, then walked to the pyre and laid the torches against it.

Heber sagged against his sons, and by chance when I looked away from him, I caught Keret, the elder priest of Baal, looking at Heber and those same sons with an expression as anguished as Heber's own.

With a shock, I remembered that Keret was the true father of Pigat's sons—sons he could never claim as his own. Sons who would not weep at his death, but at Heber's. Pigat had been his link to those sons, and now she was gone.

I turned away from him, as well, and found Achaia staring at me with silent horror.

"They're . . . burning her," she whispered. "They're burning Pigat, as if she were . . . something foul. Trash."

"What would you have them do with her?" I asked, puzzled.

"Carry her to a tomb. Lay her on a bench, cover her with a shroud, and seal the door. When her husband dies, put him in the tomb with her. When her sons die, put them in the tomb with her. How can all of them stand here and permit this desecration— her husband, her sons? How can they watch her thus reduced to ash and bone?"

Tears were rolling down Achaia's cheeks, and I hugged her close, and patted her back. "She is finished," I said. "She has left us. Her smoke rises to the gods."

"This is what they'll do to me, isn't it? When I am

78

dead, they will burn me to ash and discard me. My sons and daughters will never be able to stand outside my tomb and know that I am within. I will be truly gone, as if I had never been. Yahweh-Shalom will no longer know me."

When the fire had burned away to ash and bits of wood, with nothing left of Pigat, we returned to Heber's tent, where the women of the camp had made food for all of us. The women mourned in the women's side, the men in the men's side.

It was in mourning that I discovered the reality of my situation. The first of everything within the women's side came to me: the first bite of food, the first sip of wine. For the first time, the weight of my future settled upon my shoulders. I was now Heber's *only* wife. If he took another, I would be the new first wife. I would take over the responsibilities Pigat had handled so gracefully and so well that we often did not even notice she had done them.

She had been the one to make sure of the food—its storage, its acquisition, the amounts we would use in each meal. She it was who spoke with authority about what the house would need—purchases like wool and pots and cooking implements, dyestuffs, lamps and oil, how many other things that I had not even thought to notice?

She it was who soothed Heber when he became violent—so that what could have ended in tragedy ended only with bruises and weeping.

And now she was gone, and the mantle of her vast responsibility fell on me. I knew Heber would not believe me capable of the duties that were now mine, and in truth, I did not feel myself ready for them. I was to be mistress of the household and comforter of a man I hated? I was to be the pin that held everything together?

I had wept before for Pigat's death, but now I wept for my own loss; I wept for the death of the one barrier that had stood between me and the full force of Heber's personality. I was not a wife he loved. I was the wife of his old age, a stranger to him, a broodmare obtained for the width of my hips and the long future of childbearing I was expected to endure. He cared no more for me than he would have cared for a new goat that the seller had claimed capable of producing a goodly quantity of fresh milk every day and two strong kids each season. I would have a place so long as I produced what was expected of me, but I would never be special to him. Never liked. Never cared for.

When he looked at me, he would see only the face of the woman he had lost, and he would see that I was not her.

"Look how she mourns Pigat," I heard my neighbors whispering. "She mourns not from duty, but from grief." Even though I was an outsider, I earned their appreciation then; I had loved someone they, too, loved, and I was not celebrating my own rise in fortune—for such my situation must have surely looked to them.

They could not know that I would rather have been a concubine who could be cast out at a moment's notice than take the place of Heber's first wife, the one he had wanted.

We mourned until late in the night. I ate as people pressed food on me, I drank as they put wine into my hands and bade me drink. Achaia sat beside me, silent, still, her face etched with her horror. Talliya sometimes circulated, far more a wife of Heber than I would ever be. But her own grief was strong, and from time to time she would turn away from a comment that cut too close to the loss of the woman who had been her friend, her sometime protector. Once, completely overcome, she huddled in the far corner of the tent, her arms wrapped around herself, rocking back and forth and sobbing. Several older women surrounded her, comforting her. Eventually she calmed again, and moved once more through the throng.

We could all pretend for a time that at any moment Pigat would walk back through the tent flap, brush strands of gray hair from her forehead, and make some comment that would leave every woman in the room teary-eyed with laughter.

We could pretend. We could desire. We could wish.

But we could not change the truth.

CHAPTER

10

For a week we carried meals to Heber's side of the tent, and he bade of us leave the food and return whence we had come. He and his older sons ate in silence.

The three of us and Talliya's little ones ate quietly on our side. We were not wanted.

We dyed and spun and wove; we cooked and baked bread; we carried water and we bathed. We tended the goats, made curds and ghee, ground grain, dried fruits and vegetables against the empty season.

We did not sing, though; we did not laugh. Heber was quiet, but not a one of us thought his quiet would last. Not a one of us expected Pigat's last words to hold any weight with him or to affect us.

On the sixth day, when we took food in to Heber, he bade us sit. We sat around the pot, sharing food silently. Heber ate heavily, and he drank wine steadily. He looked from one of us to the next, and then

to his youngest boys, who curled on the rug beside
Talliya, their heads in her lap, both of them sound
asleep.

I noted him looking from Talliya to me, and back
to her, and I felt sure he would have preferred her
as a wife. I would have preferred her as his wife, too.

When he looked at me, as when he looked at
Achaia, his eyes narrowed. But he said nothing.

I did not even taste what we ate.

As we cleaned up after the food was gone, he put
a hand on my arm, and in a wine-slurred voice, he
said, "Come in unto me this night, Wife. It is time
that you resumed your other duties. For all that you
have done well enough these last days with the
household, still other things determine whether you
are a suitable wife or not."

And his gaze slipped from me to Talliya's little
ones, and then to his older sons who sat beside him.

He wanted a child of me, and he would not be
satisfied to wait longer without proof that I was with
child. If I did not give him sons, I would be of little
use to him.

It was a bitter thought. I had reached the point
where I understood that I would have to make the
acquaintance of the priest Keret or see my life get
harder and more dangerous, but my heart still re-
sisted doing what I knew I would have to do.

I was an obedient wife. A timid woman. I did not
have the strength of lions or the guile of serpents. I

did not have the courage to face the consequences of making that sacrifice with Baal's priest. Yet I was an obedient wife, and my duty to my husband was to give him sons.

And I wanted sons and daughters. Children to love me, to gather around me, to hug me and play with me and work with me, to be with me in my old age so that I could know my grandchildren, and my great-grandchildren if I were blessed to live so long. I was away from my home and my own family because my parents had given up keeping me close in order to see me do well. They would rarely see any children I had. My sister hoped to marry within Hazor, and to stay near our parents. I had hoped the same thing.

But life is not wishes; it is what happens while we're wishing.

I wanted to have children. I owed my husband children. And I could have them only by doing the wrong thing.

I offered a little sacrifice at our house shrine to Baal—grain and fresh flowers—asking on my own to be given a child by Heber. I thought of also praying to Achaia's god, but she said he did not tolerate idols, and I could not quite bring myself to turn my back on Baal, my parents' god, my husband's god, and my god through all my life to that point.

I faced Heber that night with as much courage as

I could, and put behind me as quickly as possible all that occurred. There would be no tenderness for us. No happiness. He would never see me as anyone he cared for. I had my duty, though.

He would have me come in unto him more times before my next cycle, when we might begin to guess that perhaps I was with child. I had no need to make any decision about visiting the priest Keret until then.

"Why does he not marry you?" I asked Talliya a few days later. "Why does he not make you his first wife? At least he doesn't hate you. At least he does not see you as some stupid child who offers him nothing but household services and the possibility of more children. You've already given him sons."

"We have no love between us, Heber and I," Talliya said. "He took me as concubine initially because Pigat asked him to. We were sisters. I was given to the goddess Ashtartu by my parents; when I grew too old to be a sacred prostitute, I faced a future sitting veiled by the gates, offering myself to all who came to Hazor. Pigat spoke to Heber, asking him to take me as his wife, but he would not; he did not wish to have to wife a woman who had been a prostitute. But he was willing to have me as a concubine. So my sons will not inherit as Pigat's sons will. Still"—she shrugged—"I have lived well enough these last years, and better than I could have hoped.

But I cannot imagine the nature of the disaster Heber would have to undergo for him to ever make me a wife."

I sat quietly, trying to understand what she told me. I had not *known* that Talliya and Pigat were sisters. I had suspected—I could not overlook the similarities in their appearances. I'd noticed those the first day. But Pigat had been a wife; Talliya a concubine. No one would refer to their relationship—it would be disrespectful to a wife to suggest she might be in some way connected to a mere concubine, and would suggest some honor in the status of concubine that simply did not exist. And yet they had been close. They had cared for each other, watched out for each other, guarded each other's deadly secrets.

Talliya looked at me sidelong and smiled. "You need not wish that I could supplant you as first wife. You'll do well. Your mother taught you the ordering of a household, and the work of women, and you are a credit to her. You would have made any man a good wife."

"Heber hates me."

Talliya sighed. "Heber hates the world, I think, and you are in it." She shook her head. "He cared for Pigat, and even her he treated miserably. She should have had a kind husband, as should you have. But remember, you have a rich one, who has powerful friends and the respect of other men. When you give your children fine clothes, and good sandals, and meals rich with nuts and spices and good grains and fresh fruits, remember that there are women who struggle to give their little ones a crust of bread and a handful of soaked lentils."

Achaia came into the tent, excited. She had taken over gathering the water, and so had become our source of early-morning news. "I heard by the well this morning that Heber was visited by a prince under none other than Barak, son of Abinoam. This prince in disguise paid Heber for a sword to be given in secret to Barak, so that Barak might see how our master honors his bargains. I heard that Heber has not yet made for the prince this sword, and that if the prince does not get his sword at his next return, not just our household but every household in the Kenite camp will suffer, for Barak will warn all the Israelites against buying from such dishonorable men. I also have heard that some of the smiths of the camp are on their way to talk to Heber now, to tell him that he must make things right with this man."

I did not permit even the slightest smile to cross my face, though I did glance over at Talliya. "Did you hear the name of the man who is acting as envoy?"

She nodded. "Levi of Kadesh was the name he traveled under. I have never heard of that name, but I suppose it would have been a name given him by Barak."

"Certainly," I said. "And I can understand that his sons and the others would wish to . . . *counsel* him. The honest man is honest in small ways as well as in large ones."

"Heber will be furious," Talliya said. "You cannot imagine how this will make him. That other smiths would dare to tell him how he should act with those who buy from him . . ." She closed her eyes and rubbed her temple with her fingertips.

"Will Heber hurt the prince?" I asked, suddenly afraid.

"And take a chance of losing business?" Talliya laughed. "Never. He will no doubt greet the man with welcoming arms, with a kiss to both cheeks. He will spread before this Levi the finest of foods, and make up some tale about how he was unable to meet his obligations sooner. There will be lute players and dancers, as if Heber were hosting King Jabin himself, and this prince will go away mollified and placated and give a report that will make Barak glad to send his work to Heber."

Achaia, satisfied that we were impressed with her news, took the next of the kaddim and hurried off to the well again. Talliya grabbed her little one away from the oven fire when he wandered too close, and with her matteh-lehem drew out a loaf and tossed in the next. Like Pigat, Talliya could make the bread stick to the side of the oven with a neat twist of her wrist. I had not yet mastered the technique, so my bread ended up folded over, burned around the edges, lumped on the bottom of the oven and hideous when it was drawn forth.

She glanced sidelong at me, and put the baby to her breast when he went to climb at the fire again.

"Pigat could not convince him to do the right thing," she said. "Though she tried. I passed the tale to Latiya, the biggest gossip in the camp. I knew she'd make sure everyone in the camp had heard it by morning. And so she did."

"Why?" I asked her.

"Because I did not want all of us to find ourselves poor and starving." She sighed. Then she added, "Heber won't take his anger out on this disguised prince. He will save it for us. He will shout at this prince, and at distant Barak, and at the men of the camp who dared tell him how he must behave. But he will shout that anger at us, and his hands will strike us."

We would have received the same treatment anyway, sooner or later, I told myself. If Heber were not angry about one thing, he would be angry about another, and he would take his anger out on us. It was what he did. But something good would come of this. Levi of Kadesh would have his sword.

It would be time for him to return soon, I thought. Another week, perhaps. A few more days. I had no way of knowing if he returned the same time each month, or if he simply found such time as he could to make the journey and the return trip, and took it.

I knew, though, that I was impatient for his return.

And I hoped that Talliya was right, and that when Levi arrived, Heber would treat him well, and feast him. Because if he did, then Talliya and Achaia and I would be preparing the feast. We could kill a lamb, I thought, and roast it on a spit outside the tent. We could serve foods we rarely had the opportunity to cook.

And I could see Levi again, maybe from close enough that I could see his smile, and hear his laugh. I might once again look into his eyes, and hold the way they looked back at me in my memory. I could spend the rest of my life holding on to the memories of his kindness.

CHAPTER
11

Achaia and I were washing clothes when she told me, "If this Levi of Kadesh does return, I want you to do something for me."

I had a brush and Heber's best kuttonet spread on a rock, and was splashing water on it and scrubbing at the dirt along the hem. I looked over at Achaia. "If it is in my power, I'll do for you anything that I can."

"As Heber's wife, you can perhaps speak with him. I don't know if any other men of my people will be through here—this might be my one chance. If you could—if you find an opportunity where you will not be acting improperly—ask him to take a message to my mother."

"Your mother still lives?"

Achaia put the simla she had just finished scrubbing in our rinse water. "I think so. She was not taken away by Sisera's men. Nor did I see them kill her. I think she might have managed to hide, though I can't think where."

"If I can find a way to speak with him, what do you want me to pass on?"

"Tell him to tell her that I'm alive. That I'm well. And . . . happy."

"You aren't happy."

"But I could never say such a thing to her. I could never put that burden on her. She knows only that her husband was murdered and all her daughters were taken captive. Perhaps her grown sons—my brothers—live, or perhaps they died fighting Sisera's men as my father did. For all I know, my mother believes all her children are dead. I don't know what Sisera and his men might have done to my little brother. I hope she hid him, too. But it might be that I am the only child she has left—the only person from our family other than she who still lives. How could I let her believe that I was miserable, that I've been given as concubine to a man who mistreats me and who has told me I must worship the false gods of your people, or be punished? That I live among a people who will burn my body when I die?"

She twisted the simla she had just rinsed, letting the water spatter back into the jar. Then she snapped it once and put it over one of the tent's cross-lines that kept it upright.

"I don't suppose you can. I imagine she wants her daughter to be happy, even if she can't be near you."

I knew my parents felt that way, and I had not sent word to them that Heber was a vile, foul excuse for a husband. I had managed to pass word to my mother and father, via traders heading in that direction, that I was well. They had sent word to me, in the same fashion and more than a month later, that they, too, were well.

At some point in the future, I was supposed to be permitted to go visit with them for a while. I did not know when this might happen, but the journey was long and difficult, and I could not imagine Heber being gracious about sending me any time soon.

"I want you to tell this man something else, too," Achaia said.

I nodded and waited. "Tell him to tell my mother that if she gets word that I'm dying, she has to send someone to claim my body."

I turned and stared at her. "You want me to do . . . what?"

"It will be a problem, I'm sure. If my people come here to claim my body, it could lead to fighting. I don't know that I matter enough to them that they would do that for me. But . . . Yahweh-Shalom has decreed that we are to be buried in tombs. Not burned to ash." She reached over and put a hand on my shoulder. "Please. If I am to live away from my people, please promise me that, if you can help me, you will not let my body be burned when I die."

I knew I gave her a promise I had no right offering, but I offered it all the same. I had to.

93

And then, at least for a while, I put it out of my mind. We had more pressing issues to deal with.

The men spent more and more time working, as Jabin and Sisera sent more soldiers to our camp. Sisera had over nine hundred chariots at his command, and many of them required metalwork. They were built of bent wood covered in small scales of iron, with iron banding around the top and the edges of the wheels, and with spokes of bronze, and after a battle or a raid, they ofttimes required repair. Sisera had them stationed along the roads in the kingdom where they could be used to chase down any who tried to evade paying road tolls. While collecting taxes was a less hazardous occupation overall than going into battle, sometimes axles could break during a quick pursuit, or the wooden body of the chariot could suffer if the driver tipped into an unseen hole or had his vehicle thrown into rocks. When that happened, all the metalwork needed to be hammered out and redone.

So we did more cooking in the tent, feeding not just our own men, but favored customers, as well. King Jabin was pressing for more tolls along the roads, increasing his men's activity, which in turn kept all of us busier.

It was a profitable time for us.

And with seeing Heber less, it was a pleasant time for his women. In the tent, Talliya, Achaia, and I spent our days in the comfort of work and camaraderie. With the beautiful blue rovings I'd bought, I first spun fine thread, and then wove for myself the new kuttonet I'd envisioned, in the color of the fine sapphires I had seen once in a stall in Hazor. I placed in my hair a comb of gold that would have made any woman feel like a queen. But I thought the kuttonet suited me better. It was more beautiful than I could have imagined when first I saw those balls of wool.

"It's a lovely kuttonet," Achaia told me. "It speaks of spirit, of the hand that reaches down to give comfort, strength and guidance when we reach up. When you wear it, you can remember that, if you so choose, you can be forever in the presence of God, and never alone again."

I smiled, and nodded. In truth, though, I had given less thought to her god of late. In the tent, we had a respite from the worst of Heber, and it seemed to me that everything might be well enough for me, and for both of Heber's concubines. My cycle came and went, and Heber neither made comment on the fact that I was still not pregnant nor called me to his bed to plow his seed again.

It is when things are easy that we think ourselves sufficient to the world and all its ills.

Over our evening meal one night Heber said, "I made that sneaking spy a sword such as would befit any king."

"My husband, what spy is this you speak of?" I asked him.

"There came into our camp some time ago a man of Kadesh, who told me he was a simple soldier. And so I treated him as I would any simple soldier. You know how busy we have been."

I nodded.

"Yet through various means I have discovered that he was not, in fact, a soldier, but a prince for Barak, son of Abinoam, and he came to me not in his own stead, but to test the manner in which we dealt with customers. And because we have been so busy, I have not in some four months given thought to his purchase, for we have had chariots, and swords for Jabin's men, and armor, and such things as a man in my position must hold in a preferred state."

I nodded, and did not point out that I had heard him laughing about making Levi run back and forth to Kadesh in hopes that his sword might be done. Heber would ever present himself in the best of lights, whether or not he deserved to.

"This man would have given to Barak a report on me that would have cost every smith in this camp business. And all because of some bit of trickery— had he told me from the first who it was he represented, he would have been as high on my list of priorities as any soldier of Jabin's."

Because you're a petty thief in the robes of a respectable man, and a bully as well, I thought, looking at the anger on his face and saying nothing.

"So . . . you said you made him a sword?" I asked instead.

"Yes. A sword of forged iron, as good as any I have ever made, and worth so much more than he paid me that in no way can he claim that the wait was not worth his time, or that he was not treated well. He can take back to Barak the word that the Kenites are smiths of the best caliber, that they are honest and more than fair in their dealings, and that no one could have been better served."

I smiled, thinking of Levi getting his new sword when next he arrived, and Heber saw the look on my face.

"What are you thinking?" he asked me.

"That my husband is a brilliant man as well as a talented one," I said. I put my head down and concentrated on the meal. I caught just enough of the look on Heber's face to see that my honeyed words had an effect on him. He was smiling, and it was the first time in memory that I could say he smiled because of me.

I felt oddly triumphant, and I dared to hope that through honeyed words I might make my place with him a better one, and less painful and sad. Perhaps Baal had finally answered my prayer, and turned Heber into a husband a woman might want. Perhaps Baal had softened Heber's heart, and let him see that I wanted only to please him and be a good wife to him. Perhaps Baal would give life to Heber's seed, as well, so that I might give birth to Heber's son, and present him with a child of his own loins—and so honor my own vows.

I would practice my compliments and wait another month before I considered going to the priest and asking him to make the special offering that might make me with child.

"I'll bring a lamb tomorrow for you to tend," he told me. "When this man—his name is Levi of Kadesh—returns to the camp, I'll want you to kill the lamb on that day and prepare for us a feast such as you would prepare if he were the King of Hazor. Spare nothing—present only the finest of what we have. Your part in this is important, Jael. Good food and good wine cures a world of ill feelings, and this man's report to Barak could be the difference between hunger and plenty some year."

"I understand," I told him. "Everything will be done as you have requested, my husband. I will make you proud."

That night Heber fell asleep early, so I could not try out my new resolve to lead him to care for me. But I fell asleep listening to Talliya crooning to her baby boy while the toddler slept beside her, and to the older boys on the other side of the tent talking and laughing among themselves, and I thought, *Perhaps it will all go well for me.* I could imagine myself with my own little boy in my arms, holding him close, singing to him, nursing him. Or a little girl, for perhaps Baal would gift me with a daughter. Heber had never had a daughter before—maybe she would enchant him and make him laugh the way my father's daughters had enchanted him.

Maybe a daughter would soften Heber's heart.

Maybe . . .

I dreamed happy dreams that night.

CHAPTER
12

I woke in darkness two days later to the sound of raised voices—Heber's and Talliya's.

"Why have you not yet quickened, woman?"

"I'm still nursing the baby. But I think it is not even that. I'm done, Heber. I was ever slow to quicken. But now I have passed the age of childbearing. My womb has stilled. Can you not see that?"

"Then for what do I keep you? If you cannot give me sons, why do I still feed you and give you shelter?"

"Because you still honor the promise you made my sister, that you would not cast me out but would make a place for me in your tent, and shelter me as you sheltered her."

"And now she is dead and you're still here, and I have both bad ends of the same bargain. Would that you had died! Would that she had lived!"

"Would that you were a decent man who cared

for the memory of my sister enough that you would honor your word for love of her."

"I'll honor my word so long as you give me sons, Talliya. But you're not my wife. You're nothing but a concubine, and I can turn you out at any time. Best you pray to Baal to give your womb new life, for the older boy is near old enough to come to the men's side of the tent and begin to learn his work as a smith. When he does, if you are not yet with child, best you remember what it was to be a whore."

It was not yet light. I would rise with the sounds of the crowing cock and the braying ass, as would Talliya and Achaia, and we would go about our day, but I wondered how I could face her. I had never considered that he might so easily set one of his concubines aside. He could send her away and I might never see her again, and Talliya had become as an older sister to me. A friend. How would she fend for herself. She was no longer young, and if she was beautiful, hers was a beauty born of aging well. Time had already started turning her hair gray and adding lines to her face.

She had said before that she would not go to Keret again, but now I could not see how she could not. She had no other sister, had she, with whom she might live? Her parents were dead. Surely one of Pigat's grown sons would take Talliya in—but then, Pigat's grown sons had been brought up by Heber, and if he told them that she was to be sent away, which of them would choose to defy him? Her own older sons were not yet married, and lived yet under Heber's roof. They would be able to do nothing to help her.

Beside me, Achaia turned and whispered, "You're awake, aren't you?"

"Yes," I said. "Within these walls, who is not?"

"Only Talliya's little ones, would be my guess, and that's a mercy. Poor little boys."

"It would be wrong of Heber to send her away," I said, sitting up.

Achaia pulled me back down. "It can be a bitter thing to be a concubine. Even among my people, concubines can be set aside and turned out at a whim, and left with their children to make their way in the world as best they can. Most do not treat their concubines so, but everyone knows well enough that if they choose to, they can."

"Heber promised Pigat he would care for her."

Achaia said, "He promised that young soldier he'd have a sword for him, too, and only when it looked like his poor treatment would come back to bite his hand did he do what he should have done at the beginning."

And I had a hand in him doing what he ought.

I lay in the darkness, pretending to be asleep when Talliya returned to our side of the tent. Achaia did the same. But if my body was still, my mind was not. I wondered if there were any way that I could trick Heber into honoring his promise to Talliya—or if, perhaps, that would be a bad idea. Maybe she would be better off away from the man who held her in such little regard. If she could be assured shelter and good treatment in the home of one of Pigat's sons, maybe she would be happier. And I would still be able to talk with her, and see her at the well, or in her tent.

With a sword, my meddling did not seem to cause anyone real hurt. With Talliya's life, I sensed the possibility of disaster in any steps I might take. I could not help but think of all the stories women told each other while they worked, tales passed down from mother to daughter of men and women who meddled in the gods' affairs, and who found that they were the ones most hurt by their actions.

And even if tricking Heber would never come back to sting me, how could I be sure that it would not do Talliya greater harm than letting the gods have their say unhindered?

Achaia would pray to her god for a good future for Talliya; I knew that. Achaia seemed to think that her god would aid those who did not worship him as well as those who did, if only she asked it of him.

That seemed to me an odd thing to think of a god. Our priests encouraged women to pray for ourselves. For our children. But beyond that, to permit the gods to do as they would do, and to leave bigger prayers to the men.

I rose when Heber called me to go with him, shaking off all pretense of sleep.

"I have no doubt you heard my disagreement with Talliya last night."

"Yes, my husband," I said, and kept my head down and my eyes lowered.

But he would not accept that. He lifted my chin and stared into my eyes. "This is not about her, or her fate. She or the gods will decide it. My anger now lies with you, and with that Israelite harlot given me as a gift by a friend who knew no better. I well know that some women have the secret of how they can prevent the birth of a man's sons. I know not what this secret is, but I suspect that you do, for you have been my wife for half a year, and you are not yet with child. Did you think I would not discover your treachery? Do you drink some tea? Eat some herb that keeps my seed from planting in your belly?"

"I have done no such thing, my husband. I would never. I desire sons and daughters—a house full of them."

He glared at me. "That concubine of mine taught you the secret, did she not? Taught you how you might prevent me from having what you owe me. What she owes me, too."

"There is no secret," I said, and my fear must have showed in my eyes, for his lips twisted in a cruel smile.

A woman who prevented the timely birth of her

own child by inducing a miscarriage faced execution, as would any woman who helped her. The murder of the unborn was still murder. That he had hinted I might have done such a thing—or have prevented his seed from taking hold—meant that I was in terrible danger.

His accusation, should he ever choose to take it to a priest, would spell certain death for me. My word would mean nothing, and if no one could produce the miscarried child, what of that? Heber would say I had hidden the signs of my crime. He was a man of importance; I was nothing. Everyone would believe him.

I tried hard to appear brave and honest as I stood before him, feeling the weight of his gaze crushing me. Feeling the danger in my future growing deeper, darker, and closer.

If I did not produce a child for him, he would claim it was because of something I had done. He would never even consider that he might be . . . well, a dry stalk, as Pigat had called him. After all, did he not have a long line of strong sons to prove his seed was good?

If I suggested that the priest had fathered Pigat's children, Heber would kill me where I stood. If by some horrible chance he believed me, he would kill Talliya, too, and *still* kill me.

If I did not go to the priest, as Pigat and Talliya had done, or if Baal did not make Heber's seed strong, I would be sealing my own doom. But if I went and were caught, I would be stoned as an adulteress.

From being happy, from thinking that I might after all dare to hope for a good life with this man, my husband, I had been cast into a pit of fear. I felt as if lions circled all around me, waiting to devour me as they did the criminals thrown to them by the king of Hazor on feast days.

I did not know what to do.

I did not know how I might make my lot in life better.

I did not know how I might help Talliya, or Achaia, who would surely face Heber's accusations as I just had. And I did not know how I could help myself.

In that moment, I looked down at the blue kuttonet I wore, spun from the wool that Achaia had liked, and I thought of her words.

When you wear it, you can remember that, if you so choose, you can be forever in the presence of God, and never alone again. She called her Yahweh-Shalom a hand that reached down to give comfort, strength, and guidance. If only we reached up.

She did not have a shrine for her god. No idol in front of whom I could place flowers or grain. No priest in our camp from whom I could ask a sacrifice.

If I prayed to her god, he would hear me, she said.

My gods had given me nothing.

I went outside and looked up at the blue sky, its blue reflected in my kuttonet, its color a symbol of the closeness of Yahweh-Shalom to his people.

"You don't know me," I whispered. "I'm not one of Yours. But if You'll help me, I'll turn from the gods of my people, and worship You. Help me find a way to be true to my vows to my husband, to give him the child he wants, to let me be the good wife I want to be; or if that is impossible, show me how I might escape his wrath and his false accusations. Please, Yahweh-Shalom, God of my friend, I don't know what offerings you want. So I offer myself."

No wind caught me up in it, no bright lights shimmered across the sky, no fire fell from the heavens to tell me that I'd been heard. I looked around me, and the camp looked the same, as did the people in it. I could not say that anything had changed. I could not swear that anything would get better.

But my heart felt lighter, as if suddenly I no longer carried my burden alone.

I returned to the tent, saying nothing to Achaia about what I had done. She risked enough worshipping her Yahweh-Shalom. If my husband found out that she had turned me from the gods of my people, he would kill her first and me second, and have the blessing of the priests in so doing.

No. This step I took I had to take in silence and secret.

CHAPTER
13

"I'm going to see Keret," Talliya said. She had bruises on one side of her face, and her eyes were red-rimmed from crying. "I do not want to do this, but I must. And you will have to come after me. I will tell him to look for you."

"I can't," I told her. "I swore to be faithful to Heber, to be a good wife to him."

"And when you give him a son, you will have been a good wife. If you don't, he'll claim you betrayed him anyway, and you'll die."

The two of us were making the trek back from the well with water, with Talliya's toddler running at our side, chasing lizards with a stick and laughing as if this game of his were the cleverest in all the world. Several other little boys swarmed around him as we got to our tent, and for a while he was occupied with chasing and wrestling with his friends.

"I don't want to," I said. "I . . . prayed. That I

would have a child from my husband. I prayed, and now I will wait for my prayer to be answered."

Talliya said, "You're a fool. Baal gives to his favored sons. We're women—if he has not favored Heber with good seed, we cannot hope that Baal will give him what we need because *we* ask it."

"I have prayed," I told her. "I will wait to see the results of my prayer."

But as she gathered the fresh fruit and grain for her sacrifice, I knew doubt. What she said seemed to make sense. If Baal did not care to make Heber a green stalk when Heber sacrificed and asked for sons, why would that same god, who chose not to bless Heber, bless me?

Later that day, Achaia and I were spinning red wool. The bread was done, the evening meal cooking, and we had a chance to sit and catch our breath and talk for a while.

Achaia was interested in the vehemence with which Talliya had suggested I visit the priest. I did not explain the situation to her. She would not have sacrificed to Baal to begin with; Baal's priest would not feel bound to honor any silence in her behalf, even should he agree to make the special sacrifice with her.

But Achaia's knowing would risk Talliya's life. And mine. And Talliya's and Pigat's sons.

Sitting there, I offered a prayer for Achaia, too, that

she would find a way free of Heber and back to her own people. I could not imagine how she might, but I prayed anyway.

It felt strange not saying the formal words of prayer to a god in a shrine. It felt strange speaking from my heart into silence, talking to Yahweh-Shalom as if he were a person listening to me. I could not imagine that this was a proper way to pray.

Some time later, Talliya returned, a grim set to her mouth, unrolled her mattress, and lay down upon it. "He said you could go to see him at any time, and he'll be watching for you."

I nodded. "Thank you," I told her. "I'll consider what you've suggested."

I thought about it that night, long after I should have been asleep. It would be so much easier to go to the priest and return to him until I had the child in my belly that Heber wanted than to trust in a miracle.

But I listened to my heart. My heart said, *Trust.*

In the morning, Heber called me to his side of the tent.

"Wife," he said, "the guest that I told you would be coming is almost to the edge of the camp now, with three friends."

I nodded, telling my pulse not to race and my mouth not to go dry and my tongue not to grow thick and clumsy.

"Kill the lamb," he said. "Prepare a feast enough for this sneaking coward and his friends. Make it rich enough for King Jabin, and when you are done, you and the other two anoint yourselves with oil and dress in your finest clothes, and ready yourselves to serve this meal in such a way that you do not shame me."

"Everything shall be as you have commanded, my husband." I turned and hurried out of his side of the tent, hardly able to believe that the day for which I had waited was finally upon me.

Levi was coming, and I would look upon him once more.

I told Talliya and Achaia what Heber had told me, and we began to work immediately.

Talliya was most comfortable killing the lamb; she had more experience with it than either Achaia or I. So we built a good fire beneath a roasting spit that Heber had made. It had a good wooden handle that let it be turned without much danger.

While Talliya skinned and cleaned the lamb, Achaia and I got started on the rest of the meal. We would have dried dates and figs dipped in honey, parched and roasted grains highly spiced with red peppers and green, both leavened and unleavened bread, a good stew in which to dip the bread, and doves smeared in clay and roasted on the open fire beneath the lamb; wine and milk with curds to drink.

When the clay was broken off, the birds would be defeathered and skinned, and would be tender and delicious. Ours would be a meal fit for any king.

We cooked all through the long day, and carried water so that we might bathe. The heat of late summer was a burden, and Achaia and Talliya and I all did our share of rotating the spit and basting the lamb in oil.

It seemed almost impossible that twilight should be upon us so quickly, and yet I heard Heber welcoming his guest into his side of the tent.

Then I heard Levi's voice again, and the wondrous sound of it nearly stopped my breath.

How sweet the rich tones lay upon my ears. I could close my eyes and see his smile again, as I had by the well. I could imagine him smiling at me as he had before.

I thought about his lips, his eyes, the strong, straight arrow of his nose. I thought of his broad shoulders as I finished working my hair into the combs with which I would hold it back while I served my husband and his guests.

I wore the blue kuttonet; Achaia wore rich green wool woven in a pattern of her own designing. We put on such jewelry as we had for wrists and ankles. Achaia wore her string of blue beads, as well, and I wore a headdress that had belonged to Pigat. It lay across my forehead and, along with the combs, held back my hair from my face, while the five little gold almond blossoms brushed against my skin each time I moved. I thought it pretty, and Heber had requested that I wear it for this special occasion.

Talliya alone had not dressed up. She still bore bruises on her face from Heber's anger, so she would stay in the women's side of the tent and prepare the food to be carried in to the men. We had agreed on this, because she was ashamed to be seen with the marks of her master's anger so clearly stamped on her skin.

Achaia and I alone would serve.

We would be enough.

We brought out the cook pots full of nazim and grain, the basket of bread, the lamb on its board, the doves golden brown once freed from their clay casings, the milk and the wine, the figs and dates and honey. At each new item, the men commented and made their praises of our work.

I looked at them all, seated around the food piled before them on the low table. Heber, red-faced and with a smile on his lips that never reached his eyes; his older sons solemn and distant, angry at the treatment of their aunt or mother, Talliya, but unable to say anything to Heber because Heber held complete power over all of us, including them; Levi's three friends, smiling quietly and watching everything with cautious eyes; and Levi himself. Beautiful Levi, who seemed overwhelmed by the attention he had received, and untrusting of it.

The sword in its hardened leather sheath lay beside him on the rug. He had thanked my husband for it several times, effusively.

He glanced at me and praised my cooking, and studied Achaia for just an instant before turning away; I was a little hurt not to see his beautiful smile, but I was at the same time relieved that Levi had not made any special note of me, for Heber was not a stupid man. He would have seen anything out of place between us.

"You have the gifts I brought for you," Levi said to Heber as Achaia and I were getting ready to leave the men to their eating. "But my mother sends small gifts for the women in your household, my friend."

From a woven bag he brought forth wool rovings of wondrous gold, the color of grain at harvest or the sun at the last long light of day. And after that, a blue kos, a drinking bowl of exquisite make, in a fashion I had not seen before. It was a bowl from far away, I thought—from another people than my own, but people nonetheless who loved things that were beautiful. Heber received and inspected these two gifts, thanked Levi for them, and then passed them on to us.

I touched the surface of the bowl. It was glass, and had been made by a master. I had never seen the like of it. I turned it over to see if the glassmaker had left a mark on the bottom of it, such as Achaia's father had left on his pottery, but there was nothing.

I touched the cool surfaces, thinking that Levi had brought it not for the women of the house, but for me in particular. I could not claim it as my own, for Levi could not give me a gift without giving deadly insult to my husband—but it was something that I could look at and remember that it had been his hand that brought it to me.

He said it was a gift from his mother. Perhaps the rovings were, but I had a difficult time imagining a woman sending such a fine bowl to the household of a man who had so far treated her son badly. Perhaps Levi himself had chosen it.

The rovings were, I felt confident, a woman's gift. They were an exquisite color, and the wool was soft and fine and wavy. I could imagine Levi's mother—this faraway woman I had never even seen—doing the washing of the wool and perhaps the dyeing. I could imagine her son asking her for a gift suitable for the women of a craftsman whom Levi needed to impress, and I could imagine her selecting the rovings as being good enough. If she had dyed them herself, she had skill worthy of my own people, who are the most renowned of dyers and spinners and weavers.

But the bowl was of a different nature entirely. Its rich blue surfaces, unadorned, shone beneath my fingers. I took it with me and went outside with it, and held it up to the moon. Moonlight gleamed through it, highlighting bubbles and press-lines from its making. It spoke of passion. It felt like freedom the way I imagined freedom. It whispered of places far away, of different lives, of different hopes.

It was blue, and like my kuttonet, that color would remind me of Yahweh-Shalom, and the promise I had made to Him, and the favor I had asked of Him.

I would use the kos for something special, I promised myself. Something important.

CHAPTER

14

When the men had finished eating, Achaia and I gathered up the pots and bowls and carried them back to our side of the tent. We ate quickly, the three of us, and then I said, loudly, "I'm going to get water so we can wash all these pots." And before either Talliya or Achaia could offer to do it for me, I, with one of our empty kaddim, was out of the tent and walking briskly toward the well.

When I got there, I took my good time drawing the water, hoping against hope that Levi might find a way to leave my husband's company, if only for a while.

And indeed, as I was finally drawing up the heavy jar by the rope through the handle, I heard the voice I had so longed to hear.

"Let me do that for you. It's far too heavy for such a delicate creature as you, little dove."

Levi pulled the water out of the well with ease, and said, "We have set up our camp outside of yours, and we are returning to our tent now. I needed some water for myself, and for our donkeys. How fortunate I am to have chanced upon you."

"The luck is all mine," I said. "For I have a thing to ask of you which I could not ask at all, save that the woman for whom I ask it is in desperate danger."

"You do not ask a favor for yourself?"

"No. For Heber's concubine, Achaia. She was the young woman who served the feast with me. She is of your people, and has taught me to pray to your Yahweh-Shalom, and to turn away from the gods of my own people."

He nodded, the smile that had set his face alight suddenly gone.

I spoke low and fast, for fear that I might be caught. "The general Sisera stole her and her sisters away from their parents, and killed her father in doing so. Her mother may still live, but may think that all her daughters have died. Achaia's request was that someone tell her mother, who is Dara, and who lives in Beth-Anath, that Achaia still lives and that she is happy and does well." I looked around quickly. We were still alone, but I suddenly feared for myself, for what I did next I could not excuse. Nor would my husband excuse it, were I found out, or any man who knew my husband.

"In truth, however, Achaia is neither happy nor safe," I said. "She is in great danger, for my husband despises Yahweh-Shalom, and Achaia will not turn away from the worship of Him to embrace the gods of our people. And she will not be able to give my husband sons, for reasons I cannot say. Also, Heber does not like us—*her. Her.* He does not care for Achaia, and before long, Heber will find an excuse to turn her loose to fend for herself, or he will find an excuse to kill her. And if he kills her, her body will be burned, which she says your people forbid. I know I ask too much of a man who owes me nothing, but if you could . . . find it in your heart . . . to send word to her uncles or the men of her village of her danger. . . ."

Levi was studying me with eyes that saw too much. Looking at my face, my clothes, the movement of my hands as they twisted the cloth of my kuttonet.

"I suspect that there are many favors you could ask of me, and were they in my power, I would grant them all for you. I suspect that you say as much about your own life to me as you say about your husband's concubine's life. And yet you ask nothing for yourself," he said softly. "Only for the woman who is of my people."

"I . . . am married. I have . . . prayed for answers, and your Yahweh-Shalom may choose to hear my prayers."

He nodded. "Then I will do as you ask." He started to turn away, then said, "Know you by chance how it came to pass that I paid for a sword of bronze, and came to receive a sword of finest forged iron? Or to be feted in the fashion of a prince of Hazor, when I am a common soldier and much despised by your husband."

I nodded. However, I said nothing.

"Would you care to tell me how this miracle came to pass, if you know?"

I shook my head.

"But you had something to do with it, did you not, little dove?"

I looked around, furtive and frightened, but still the night wrapped its wings around us like a mother bird around her young, and gave us that little time alone. "I did," I whispered.

And then I said, "I must go. I cannot stay here. I wish you well. A safe journey, and happiness, and all that is good in life."

I drank in the way he looked, there in the deep shadows, his strong features picked out and highlighted by moonlight. It was going to be the last time I saw him, so I took a second or two longer than I should have—but this look would have to last me a lifetime.

Finally, however, I turned away, and picked up the water-filled kad, and balanced it atop my head, and walked slowly back to Heber's tent, where Talliya and Achaia had finished feeding the remaining scraps to Heber's dog.

They did not ask me why I had tarried so long, nor did I offer any explanation then. When I was alone with Achaia later, though, I said, "Your message is on its way to the ears that need to hear it."

She hugged me. "Thank you. Thank you. My mother will have some peace, I hope, knowing that one of her children still lives and thrives."

"She will," I said. "I have faith."

It was true. I did have faith—that Levi would get the message through, that Achaia's mother would still be alive to receive it. And that, somehow, in some fashion, some of her people would find a way to get her home.

The hot, dry days stretched endlessly before us, and the work the camp smiths did got heavier, harder, and more urgent. Rumors of a pending war assailed us, of the Israelites moving in the highlands, raiding Canaanite caravans and evading Canaanite tax collectors. Blockades failed to stop them, and the chariots racing across the flatlands found themselves increasingly thrown into dug and hidden traps as the blockade runners lured them off their safe paths.

Sisera became a frequent visitor to the camp as he checked on work done and work remaining to be done; he ate in our tent far more often than either Achaia or I would have liked. Talliya didn't mind him so much, but she was to old to attract his attention, or his comments, made to Achaia and me when he was sure no one else could hear him.

Sisera was a general. A powerful man. If he had asked Heber for the loan of either of us for a night,

I almost doubt that Heber would have refused us to him.

He had no time for us, though, thankfully. We got through the majority of our dyeing and spinning, the weaving, the sewing, and after that, the harvesting of the small patches of grains our people raised for ourselves, and the threshing and hulling and grinding of our own grain and the grain we'd bought. It was hard labor, backbreaking and dull. Women's work or slaves' work—and there are times when I think there is no true difference between the woman and the slave—but of the least pleasant kind. We sang while we worked, and told stories as best we could to keep our minds off the hard labor, but we fell onto our straw mattresses come full dark each night and did not stir again until the next daybreak.

I was grateful that Heber had no time for me. He had no time for Talliya, either, or for Achaia.

In fact, he had so little time for us that when Talliya declared that her visit to the priest had borne fruit, and that she was with child, I asked her if she had been with Heber at the right time for him to think the child his own.

"Barely," she said, "but he thinks well enough of himself that he'll be willing to credit that one night together as sufficient for the cause."

She became sick, of course—unable to bear the smell or taste of food, ever turning to a small, cheap pot she always kept in a corner to be sick in. She grew quiet, and thin, and tired-looking, as well. Achaia and I did her work as well as our own, while she lay on her mat and slept for hours on end.

We worried about her as the weeks passed and the sickness didn't. We encouraged her to drink milk, and brought it to her fresh. We fixed foods without spices for her, and made extra unleavened bread, because bread she could keep down better than most other things.

Her two little ones we tended, as well. We even saved extra goat's milk for the smallest so that Talliya could wean him—nursing him had become too much for her.

She didn't complain. She didn't say much of anything. It almost seemed to me that something inside her had broken.

We gave her rovings, and her spindle and distaff, and when she could sit up at all, she spun a bit, making thicker threads and yarns suitable for clothes that would protect against the coming wet season.

"There," Heber said one day when, sweating and stinking, he threw himself to the ground and dug into the food without having first washed. "There is what a woman is supposed to be." And he pointed at Talliya. "Quiet, obedient, pregnant." He patted her hand in a proprietary fashion; I'd seen him make the same gesture toward his dog, or toward a favored goat.

That was what we were to him. Goats. Livestock,

useful so long as we produced and didn't start kicking or biting.

He hadn't had cause to accuse either Achaia or me of wrongdoing in the past month or so. If I found myself pregnant at that point, it would have been a disaster and a sign of infidelity rather than a reason for him to swagger among the other men announcing that he had another son on the way—and that he knew it would be a son because he made only strong boys.

I found it hard to school myself not to hate him for that. Not to despise him. He was a braggart and a bully, a man willing to curry favor with those more powerful while abusing and using those weaker than himself.

He had a talent that few men could claim, and he was a master of that talent. Yet somehow, he had taken his gift and twisted it. He believed that he was the equal of kings and generals, the friend of the powerful and the dangerous. He walked with lions, but he was no lion. He was at best a jackal, feeding off the carcasses when the bigger beasts were done, trailing along in their company, tolerated by them because he had not yet done anything to anger them.

I did not want to see what would happen to him if he did anger them. Or perhaps I did.

I did *not* want to see what would happen to *us*, though, if he managed to turn his powerful associates against him, since our fates were bound with his.

"You're quiet," Achaia said.

We were taking turns grinding grain into flour on the rehayim, our household hand mill, and I was catching my breath while Achaia rocked back and forth, pushing the pelah rekeb, the upper stone, called the "rider," over the grain that lay in slightly hollowed-out surface of the pelah tahtit, or "saddle quern." We were grinding barley and hard wheat, emmer, and bread wheat, and storing our ground flours in kaddim, so the rhythm of our work consisted of pressing down and pushing, grinding, lifting up the heavy stone, pouring the contents into the correct kad, lifting up a heavy kad with unground grain in it, pouring, and then repeating.

The day had a faint hint of coolness in the air, perhaps a harbinger of the rainy season, but both of us were so hot and tired after half a day of this labor that we could barely move.

Still, I answered Achaia before I returned to my turn on the hand mill. "It occurred to me that Heber has made enough enemies that, should his few friends desert him, you and I and Talliya will have a very hard life."

"He's rich."

"I know that. But I was thinking about how quickly riches can fall away. How fortunes can change in an instant."

"As mine changed when Sisera and his men raided our village."

I nodded. "As mine changed on the day I married Heber."

"If fortunes change for ill, they can as quickly change for good," Achaia said softly.

I looked at her sitting there, waiting her turn at the hand mill. "I have already prayed to your Yahweh that they will."

I should have seen it coming. Men cannot work so hard and drink so heavily without something going wrong eventually.

But I was weary. Achaia was, too. And Talliya had grown almost sticklike around the rising swell of her belly, and was far too weak to help us with the burdens Heber, his sons, and the steady stream of Sisera's men imposed upon us. I did not watch Heber as closely as I should have—though even had I watched, I was not certain that I could have averted the storm that came.

We had not known that we were to be entertaining and feeding yet more men. We had prepared for that night's meal dishes with barley, plain and simple fare that was most often considered the food of the poor, or even feed for the animals. But I was no expert in figuring the amount of food we would need for the ever-changing numbers of men we fed, and I had not purchased wheat in sufficient quantities the last time a trading caravan came through.

I was new to being the woman in charge of the household, and I had no one to help me; even Talliya had never purchased the food before. She tried to help, but she knew no more about the amounts we might need or how to figure in advance for extras at our table during this busy season than I had.

So when my husband brought home customers who had brought their chariots for repairs—weary warriors who had traveled far and through difficult terrain to reach us, and who would be guests of our house for at least the night, and perhaps a second day—I had nothing with which to present them but the last of the bread made of wheat, and a porridge of barley and onions, the same sort of food that they might have found in the house of a poor man.

And there was my husband, shamed by the poor hospitality he gave them. In front of them at the meal, he did nothing but glare at me. However, from the storm in his eyes, I knew that he would have words and more with which to chastise me after all had been fed.

Nor would I gain any grace from him for being inexperienced as the matriarch of our household. He had paid a great deal for me, and I had left him humiliated in front of warriors. *Warriors*.

I dreaded the moment when he would call me in to speak with him.

But he didn't call me to his side of the tent.

He came to ours as we washed the cooking pots following the meal.

"Goat feed," he snarled without preamble. "You prepared for me goat feed. And for Jabin's fighters—goat feed. And for my sons—goat feed."

It had been a tasty meal. Not, certainly, the fare of the rich, but well spiced, with olives and olive oil for seasoning, with fresh black grapes on the side, which in that season were plentiful and lush and delicious.

But I hung my head. For days I had been waking before first light, hoping to find that another caravan had come, because I knew we were nigh out of wheat, and I hoped to make a large purchase so that we would never be short again.

And no caravan had come. One had been on its way to us, according to the warriors we'd fed only the day before, but raids and rumors of war had turned them back, and no one was certain when the next caravan would dare the roads and the possible raiding parties in the area around Mount Tabor to bring us supplies.

It is one of the difficulties of living in a tent village that farming is so often futile, since the camp as a whole must be ready to pick up at any time to follow work. We'd grown a little of our own grain that season, but lentils and barley had done better than wheat, so our long stay hadn't helped me.

I said, "Forgive me, my husband. I did not expect

the number of guests we would feed when last the caravan was here with grain to purchase. We ran through our stores of wheat, and I did not know that we would have guests for our meal this night."

"It is your duty to ensure that each mouth in this household is fed," he said, and, when I started to say that they had been, held up his hand to silence me. "Your duty." His voice began to rise. "Do you *hear* me? Do you *hear* me?* If we do not have adequate food to feed our guests well, you bring shame upon me. Our hospitality is a mark of our quality. A successful smith does not feed his guests food fit only for animals; neither does his wife feed him animal food, if she would have a long and happy life."

Pigat would have talked to him—she would have said something that soothed him and comforted him. She would have found a way to calm him, to drain the violence from him. Of course, Pigat would never have let the household run out of wheat, either. She would have purchased extra.

"I failed you. I will do better, my husband," I said, hoping that contrition and an admission of my guilt would appease him.

But he lifted one of the cook pots we had just finished cleaning and threw it to the ground so hard, it smashed. Potsherds flew everywhere.

"You did fail me, you worthless excuse for a wife. You have not yet given me a son, nor do you show any signs of having caught, but I assured myself that you could weave and you could dye and you could sew, that your cooking was acceptable, that you could milk and make cheese and grind grain and those other duties of women. That you were not completely without value. I told myself these things, but they were not true."

He picked up another of our cook pots and smashed it into the ruins of the first.

A piece of pottery tore past me, brushing my skin. I felt a sharp stab of pain, and when I put my hand to my cheek, it came away bloody.

Achaia, who had been crouching against the back tent wall, hiding, jumped forward at that and touched my cheek.

She looked accusingly at Heber, while I prayed that she would say nothing and crawl back into her corner, but she rose to her feet and shouted at Heber, "You hurt her! You cut her. She's bleeding."

Heber did not even waste a word on Achaia. He grabbed her by the necklace of blue beads she wore and used them to yank her toward him. At the same time, he balled up his fist and hit her once in the belly, and when she started to topple, once in the face.

She collapsed to the floor and lay still. Talliya shrieked in spite of herself, and Heber said, "Shall I come to you, too, woman? Would you protest my right to punish those who live under my roof and at my mercy?"

Talliya shook her head slowly, her eyes huge in her face. She said nothing.

"I would that my reputation had some value to you, stupid girl. I would that I could assume that after a day of hard work I could come home and find food intended for men waiting for me."

"I made a mistake. But I won't make it again."

His eyes narrowed. "You won't," he agreed.

My heart constricted, and my breath almost could not find the path to my lungs. He looked at me with eyes like death. He looked down at Achaia, who lay silent and still as a pile of rags on the floor by his feet.

I saw no pity, no mercy, no compassion there. I saw only disgust and drunken rage.

And then he bent down, lifted another pot, and smashed it to the floor. And after it, another. And after that, another, until every piece of cookware that we had lay in shards and shatters upon the ground. I expected him to go after our drinking bowls, our serving ware, and our storage pottery next, but he did not.

Instead he said,"You'll cook good food tomorrow. Food fit for people. If you don't, I'll make you wish you had never been born."

I believed him.

He stormed from our side of the tent, leaving a costly ruin and the still, bloodied form of Achaia behind him.

When he was gone, Talliya unrolled Achaia's mattress, and we got Achaia moved onto it. She was still breathing; I was relieved. I had feared for her life.

Talliya soaked a rag in water and mopped the blood from the girl's nose and mouth, then lay it on her forehead.

Her nose swelled to twice its size, her lips—cracked and bloody—did the same, and the skin under her eyes went puffy and black. When at last she came around enough to look at us, the first sound from her mouth was a whimper.

"You fool," Talliya whispered. "Never, never stand up to him like that. Always bow your head, always keep your eyes lowered, always stay out of his reach. What did you think he was going to do to you when you shouted at him? He *owns* you. You have no right to speak to him in such a fashion. He could have killed you right then, and we would have been left to build a pyre for you—or if he was particularly angry, he could have had you dragged out to the ravines and thrown you over the side, so that vultures and wild dogs could fight over your bones. And no one would have worried that a concubine was dead. No one would have questioned how you had come to die, no one would have cared."

"I know," Achaia whispered.

"Promise me," Talliya said, glaring, "that you will never again do such a foolish thing."

"He hurt Jael," Achaia said. "Her face is all covered with blood."

My hand flew back to my cheek. I had forgotten about my injury.

I could feel my skin, sticky with my own blood, and once I remembered it was there, the sharp sting of the cut on my face.

Talliya handed me another water-soaked rag and waited while I cleaned my face.

Then the three of us surveyed the ruins of our pottery.

He had not destroyed the kaddim that held our grain and water. Our drinking bowls. Our serving platters. But every single cook pot lay shattered in the broad-scattered pile of potsherds on our floor.

I closed my eyes. "How are we to cook a meal tomorrow? We have barley, but no wheat left. We have no pots in which to cook. We have no way to bake bread. We have almost nothing. What are we to do?" And then I turned at the little cry of dismay Achaia made, and saw her staring at the potsherds.

It didn't hit me for an instant. When it did, it felt almost as though Heber had punched me in the belly.

The buqbuq her father had made lay in the ruins.

"Oh, no," I whispered. I picked my way through the sharp edges of fired pottery, brushed a clear space for myself in the center of the area of greatest ruin, and began picking my way through the devastation, looking for any part of that one pot that I might save for her.

My search was rewarded, eventually, though I paid for it with cuts on my fingers. I found the better part of the bottom of that pot intact—and the bird design on it almost perfect. The tip of one wing had chipped away, but the rest was fine.

I rose and carried it to her, and tried not to let my eyes fill with tears as she clutched it to her breast and began to weep over it.

"Lie down. Sleep," I told her. "We'll clean up the mess, Talliya and I. Press the cloth to your face, and be still for a while."

Still crying, she nodded, and turned her back to us and lay on the mattress. I could see her shoulders shaking as she sobbed.

Poor girl. She had been hurt for my sake.

Inside me, something shifted; I knew that I had changed, and would never again be as I had been before.

I hated Heber. I still wanted to get Achaia away from him. But now I wanted to get myself away from him, too. Now I was determined that I would find my way to freedom from him. No longer would I try to convince myself that my duty was to be his good wife.

My duty was to survive, and I could see a darkness in my future that terrified me. If I stayed his wife, I would die by his hand.

I did not want to die.

I hoped that Achaia was right about the One God listening to any who asked for His aid. I intended to entreat Him with everything in me to save us.

I did not know how He might do such a thing. I could not be sure that I even *believed* that He could do such a thing.

I knew only that I could not.

CHAPTER
16

I spent much of the night praying, lying on my side on my mattress, listening to the others sleep. I did not know how we would cook meals without cookware. How we would find wheat to serve instead of barley. How we would stay safe from Heber.

I could do nothing, so I put everything I could not do into the hands of Yahweh-Shalom.

And at last, feeling lighter, I closed my eyes and slept.

We woke early, to the sound of light footsteps beside our tent, and the voice of Ahm-Amat, wife of one of Pigat's sons, asking if she might enter.

"I could not help but hear the noise last night," she said. "And, oh, dear gods, Achaia, your *face!* I saw the shards of all your cook pots and your tannur on the ground, so that you cannot bake your bread. Something woke me this morning to come to see if you needed anything; obviously, you do."

Was that how He worked, the One God of Achaia's people? Was this the answer to a prayer?

As I was Heber's wife, Ahm-Amat addressed her question to me. I said, "We've been feeding so many, we ran out of wheat. I did not know to order so much this season."

"It isn't usually like this," Ahm-Amat said. "And you have borne the brunt of guests. We have so few in our tent. I have extra wheat, and I'm sure some of the others do, as well. If we each give you a little, you should have enough, and we won't go without, either." She smiled.

"We have not a single cooking pot remaining," I told her.

"I saw." She thought for a moment. "Latiya on the other side of the camp got a new tannur, while her old one was still serviceable. The new one has black birds and a red slip coating on it—she said she saw the pretty birds and she just had to have them." Ahm-Amat rolled her eyes. "But her extravagance bodes well for you. And I'm sure that Donatiya has more pots than she uses, since it's just her and her husband now, and all their children are out and have tents and families of their own. Surely there must be others within the camp who have a pot they aren't using."

"Thank you," I told her. "And blessings on you." I didn't say whose.

She smiled at me. "We're family," she said. "I would not leave you to hurt the way you are. And . . ." She shook her head, her dark hair swinging. "Heber. He was different when he was younger, I heard. But I've never known him to be different, and I must admit that I think he has ever been the sort of man we all see now. I simply think that while he still had Pigat, he had moments when he rose above who he really is."

I hugged her, and she hurried off.

"You can't go out," I told Achaia. "Your poor face is a disaster. And"—I looked at Talliya—"you definitely can't carry water, the way you've been. So I'll get the water quick as I can, and perhaps we'll have at least a pot and something to cook in it by the time I'm finished."

"I'm taking the potsherds beyond the camp to the ravine and throwing them in," Achaia said.

Something about the way she said it made the hairs on my arms stand up. I shivered. "Wait for me. I'll go with you. The jackals often lurk there, hoping to find scraps. You dare not go alone."

"I would dare," she said, and I caught the defiant edge to her voice.

I suspected that she had decided to run away.

If she did that, Heber would have every right to hunt her down and kill her.

"Wait," I said. "Talliya, make sure she waits."

Talliya seemed to catch the urgency in my voice. She gave Achaia an odd look and said, "She'll be here when you return."

I hurried. Four large kaddim of water I needed to fill, and the well was crowded. Many of the women there had become my friends, and had already heard from Ahm-Amat about our plight with pots and wheat. They told me that they had sent their little ones to our tent already, carrying whatever they could spare.

It sounded like we would end up with more pots than we had started with. And perhaps more wheat.

"Many hands make the burden lighter," more than one said.

I could not disagree.

When I'd filled the fourth kad, I carried it back, my heart lighter than it had been in days. Something in me had changed, but something in the wind had changed, too. Something in the lay of the light across the land. Something in the morning, something in the whole of the world. I could feel good things coming.

Talliya echoed my optimism. She was sitting beside our tent, the outside walls were already lifted for the day, and she was baking bread, a half-smile on her face.

"The oven is here already," she said. "And I don't feel sick. In fact, I feel hungry."

"Good," I told her, grateful and relieved that she had an appetite. That was the best news I had heard in a very long time; if she could eat and keep down food, she might get fatter before the baby was born, which would be good for both her and the baby.

We roasted wheat on a mahabat—a flat pottery griddle—and served that with lehem and curdled milk, and Heber did not comment on the food or where we might have gotten it, or how we might have prepared it. It was as if he had expected us to be able to cook on nothing and feed him wheat from the air.

Or perhaps he had been so deeply lost in the wine that he did not remember the night before.

Well, *he* might not have. But we did.

I could barely look at his face. I could only think that if I could not escape him, I would be looking at that face for the rest of my life—which, since I would not be having his child, would be a short one.

We did not speak as we ate, and Talliya, Achaia, and I cleared everything away in silence. The men went off to work.

It was not much later, while Achaia and Talliya were visiting one of Pigat's daughters-in-law in her tent and I sat spinning, that I heard Heber return.

With him, I heard the booming, obnoxious voice of the general Sisera.

Sisera's voice dropped when they were within the tent.

"We are soon to carry our war against Barak, son of Abinoam, who has been moving troops into the highlands at Mount Tabor. I wish to ask of you a favor, for you and your sons only."

"You know you have only to ask, and what is mine to give is yours to receive."

"I would ask of you, then, that without word of where you are going or why, you take yourself and your fine sons to Elon-bazaanannim, that is, Oak in Zaanannim. Quietly move your camp away from the rest of the Kenites, and set up there so that you will be out of the battle but close enough to my men that you can get our weapons in good repair as we head into battle and as we fight."

"You know I will do this thing for you; it is the matter of a moment. You are my dear friend; should you ask it of me, we will pack up all that we own and be gone this very night."

"It is exactly that which I do ask." Sisera's voice dropped lower, and I leaned closer to the dividing cloth between the women's side of the tent and the men's. "In this battle, we have a chance to destroy the thorn that has been in Jabin's side for twenty years. We have made mighty sacrifices before Baal. His altars have run with blood. The augurs have cast our fortunes and have declared for us a massive and long-awaited victory. But we would not have these plans known to our enemies, who come to the Kenites for their weapons, just as we do. If you and yours are hidden away, with nothing said to anyone, all our fortunes are sure to rise together."

I heard Heber give a soft chuckle. "Indeed. Let us then share wine and offer our libation to the gods, who shall oversee this victory."

I leaned back, the spindle in my hand moving without my thought, the thread spinning out with a life of its own. My mind settled on the fact that there was to be a battle between Sisera and my people, and Barak . . . and Achaia's people. A battle in which Levi of Kadesh would fight for the people I was almost bound to think of as my enemy.

Except I didn't. My family were not fighters. My mother and sisters were dyers and spinners, my father and brothers master weavers. They had no stake in this fight. I did. Achaia was my stake. Her people would be nearby, perhaps. We would be out of the battle, but close enough to keep weapons in good repair, Sisera had said. Close enough to Sisera's men meant close enough to Barak's, as well, didn't it?

If we were to be that near the Israelites, we would be close to armed fighters who might be able to steal Achaia away—to make her the spoils of war for a second time, and get her home again—if only they knew to look for her.

But I had no way to get word to Levi, to ask him to pass on to her people this place where she would be.

It was such a lovely thought, though. To have them race in with swords drawn and spirit her away from Heber.

Perhaps they could take me, too.

I thought I would be willing to be a concubine to an Israelite man, if he were like Levi.

I did not allow myself to consider that Levi himself might take me off to be his captive. It was a shameful thought for a married woman to have, even one who hated her husband and wished herself anywhere but where she was.

I did, in truth, spend a few moments in that fantasy, but my fingers still spun good wool, so it was not as if I sat idly.

Talliya and Achaia returned not long afterward. Sisera and Heber were gone by then, and we had the tent to ourselves. I told them what I had heard, and what I thought about Achaia. Any fancies I had of my own rescue, I kept to myself.

"It answers the question well enough of what is to become of you," Talliya said to Achaia when she had heard the whole of my tale. "We'll find a way to get word to your people that you are there and in need of rescue."

Talliya had a new and fierce resolve about her that seemed to have come to her with the return of her appetite. It suited her.

Achaia gave both Talliya and me a grateful smile. "You're wonderful, my sisters. Yahweh-Shalom bless you both."

"My concern," I said, "is that we will have no opportunity to get word to the ears of those who need it. We must leave tonight, and if no caravans find us once we are in this Oak at Zaanannim, not only will we have no chance to buy more wheat or replace these borrowed cook pots with purchased ones of our own, but we will have no chance to tell anyone who would care to spirit her away where Achaia will be."

"Leave that to me," Talliya said, and turned and hurried out of our tent, in the direction of the well.

"Do you think—?" Achaia started to say, and she wore a bright and hopeful smile on her face.

I held up a hand to silence her. "Say nothing more about it. Not a word. What can be done will be done, but we must begin packing. We'll have to be ready to leave when darkness comes; Heber intends to have us steal away like thieves in the night. Talliya will have to sleep. I have no idea where this Oak in Zaa-nannim is, but she is in no condition to be up and packing during the day, and walking all night."

"Poor Talliya. Won't he at least give her a donkey to ride?"

"Heber? Why would he? He wouldn't give the goats an ass to ride. We are to him nothing more than goats. We serve his purpose."

She looked at me with sorrowful eyes, but turned her attention to putting away our weaving and spinning, and locating ropes for the jars of our stores, that we might fit them into Heber's wagon.

CHAPTER
17

In blackest night we walked before the goats, but behind Heber. The three of us had Heber's sons around us, armed with swords and spears and hammers. They were strong men with strong arms, and once we were outside the perimeter of the Kenite camp, two chariots, each holding three men and drawn by four horses apiece, joined us. Sisera had given us an escort to see us safely over the roads and through the darkness.

I hated to admit it, for I loathed Sisera, but I was grateful for the escort. We had no moon overhead, and little of the light of the stars. Walking in darkness through the wilderness is a terrifying thing. Lions and bears and jackals live in the wilderness. So do thieves and murderers.

The men talked loudly, so we talked softly in our little cluster, and were not overheard.

"I managed to tell one of Barak's men, who was

getting water for his trip out of camp, where we would be, and that we had a daughter of Beth-Anath in our midst who had been stolen away from her parents and was being ill-treated. He promised that he would spread the word among Barak's men, and if the battle went in their favor they should come and take her away from Heber,'' Talliya reported.

"We pray, then, for Sisera's defeat."

"I've been praying for that for years," Talliya said. "Jabin has other generals who are not such swine. But for some reason that I shall never understand, he favors Sisera above them all."

The road was uneven, and Talliya tripped. We caught her, but she cried out.

She was not yet great with child, not nearing her time. Still, I worried for her, that she might hurt herself or the unborn babe. This was madness, I thought, to travel by night with five camels, five families, a huge flock of goats, the young goatherds, all our food, our homes, everything we owned in the world.

If bandits hit us, we would be destitute.

An owl hooted nearby. I shivered. It is a mournful sound. Not far away, jackals yipped and howled. At some distance, a lion roared.

The men kept their weapons at the ready, the goats trotted together, in close and nervous, and we three women held hands and shivered, and decided to move back with the wives of Heber's sons. Achaia and I took turns carrying Talliya's toddler and the baby, who were sleepy and who spent most of the journey with their heads bobbing on our shoulders.

Back with the daughters-in-law, we found ourselves gossiping and telling stories to keep our minds off the long walk, and the darkness, and our own fear. We told women's tales, of husbands outwitted by their wives' cleverness, of young women who thought themselves better than the gods, of gods who fancied mortal women and took them to wife, usually with heartbreaking results.

"I have a story," Achaia said. "A true one."

She had said nothing through most of the tales, laughing with the rest of us at the follies of men and the ways that women could work them to their wills, but she had not offered much commentary.

So we were all interested to see what sort of story she thought worthy.

"Once, not so terribly long ago, my people were slaves of the pharaohs in Egypt," she said.

And she told us of the young man, rescued from a slaughter of firstborn sons, raised by the daughter of a pharaoh, who grew up, found the god of his own people, and found himself set against those he had once been a part of.

In her tale, I heard some of my own life. Certainly I was no hero, as this Moses she spoke of had been. I did not face a pharaoh, offering threats of plagues, or see those plagues carried out. I did not lead my people through a sea with the water towering around us on all sides, nor did I see that same water pour down and swallow my enemies and their horses and chariots when we had all reached safety.

But like Achaia's Moses, I knew the voice of Yahweh-Shalom. He spoke in my heart, telling me—when I dared listen—that I could save this daughter of His. That I could serve Him, and be one of His people, whom He loved.

I walked through the darkness with the others, thrilled and horrified by Achaia's story, and I wondered, if I dared to serve, how her Yahweh would use me.

We pitched a tent during the hottest part of the day, and all of us slept beneath it, with the women making a simple meal and the men taking turns to keep watch over the animals and the campsite. As we could, we slept, too.

When we'd had a little sleep and the worst of the day's heat had passed, we got up and moved on.

It was a hard march, repeated through the whole of the night, and then the following night, as well.

But at last we reached Oak at Zaanannim. It was lovely. The tree for which the place had been named was tall and broad-spreading, its branches open in embrace, its leaves offering cooling shade. The spring flowing into a deep well full of water was both sweet and cold. The rest of the ground was also covered with trees, the outlying areas rich with good graze for the animals, and we found many pleasant spaces in which to pitch the tents.

I liked the place. I thought, if I were to live not in a civilized town but in the wilds for the rest of my days, that it was a very fine place to live.

We would not stay there, of course. We would go where work took us. Probably, after this was done, back to the main camp, and then on around the countryside, from town to town and city to city.

Everyone arrived dirty and weary, but no rest awaited us. Usually the men would set up the tents while the women unpacked and began preparing food, but Sisera was waiting for the men when we arrived, and with him a host of warriors with armor and weapons and chariots needing service. So the wives and daughters pitched the tents and set up the camp. We know our way around ropes and tent pegs and mallets; we are strong and sturdy. We had the camp set up quickly enough, and our belongings unpacked and in place, with rugs on the ground and food stores set up. We sent the children to gather fuel, we set up our ovens and our hand mills, and we began to cook. Food always comes first, then such luxuries as sleep.

I thought, grinding meal for nazim full of olives and red peppers, that after such a journey I should like to be able to sleep for days and nights without moving. I suspected my husband would work himself to exhaustion, eat, drink his wine, and be asleep, bothering neither me, Talliya nor Achaia, for the whole of the time that Sisera was preparing his army for battle.

It was something for which I could be grateful, and I was. If it kept him away from us, I would not begrudge the extra work we did.

But we were not to have rest that night, either.

The sound of a sharp scream woke me.

My first thought was that Heber had taken his fists to Achaia again, but this time we women were alone within our side of the tent.

Talliya clutched her belly. "Too soon!" she screamed. "Too soon."

I ran to her side and rested my hand on her round stomach, and felt it harden like stone beneath my palm. "No," I whispered.

"Yes," she said. Her face ran with sweat.

"How long has this been going on?"

"It woke me only moments ago. It has just started, I think."

"The midwife is back in the main camp."

She nodded. "Bring the other women, as many as can come. None are midwives, but most have assisted. One of them has a birth-chair, I think. If not, we'll tie a rope to the—" She threw her head back and screamed again.

Heber shouted from the other side of the tent that we were disturbing him. I shouted back that Talliya's time had come. That silenced him.

I sent Achaia running for the other women in camp, those few who might have slept through both Talliya's screams and my shouts.

They came bringing a birthing chair, and rags, and a clean silver knife to cut away the placenta. They brought gifts for the little gods in their shrines, to ask for a live birth and a healthy baby, though this was, we all feared, too soon, and their prayers were unlikely to be answered. I prayed in my heart to Yahweh-Shalom all the same, and knew Achaia did as I did.

Talliya had been sick for so long, though, and this baby would be early and small. There was little hope for any of us, and much fear for the baby's life, as well as hers.

She lay still and we tried to soothe her, hoping that her labor would cease. One of Heber's daughters-in-law brewed her a tea thought to calm the angry womb, but even though we kept her lying on her side, and she sipped at the tea, the baby would not be stopped in his progress.

And the birth, when it came, came fast. She sat upon the chair, and the women knelt with hands beneath it and received the little baby, who did not cry. We had known, I thought. One tied the cord, one cut it, and the placenta came quickly, too. Someone handed the child to me, and I wrapped it in a cloth. The cloth would be its shroud, I thought.

And remembered something I had seen the midwife do with the birth of my youngest brother, who did not cry. She had picked him up by his ankles and smacked him once, sharply, on his little behind. He had not cried. So she had put her mouth over his nose and mouth and breathed into his lungs. Just a little, I thought, for a baby has such tiny lungs. But in a few moments, he had cried. And he had lived.

I could do that, I thought. I did what I had seen the midwife do. Several of the women stared at me, and one gasped in horror.

But within moments, the baby gave its first cry, a thin, high wail that silenced every voice in the room.

I started to weep. Around me, women quickly handed the child to its mother, and Talliya put the babe to her breast. The infant, after a moment, began to suck.

"She's had a girl," Achaia whispered in my ear. "Everyone says this is the first girl born to Heber or any of Heber's sons. And she lives."

"A daughter," I thought. Someone with whom to share spinning and weaving and cooking, a child she would get to keep, who would not be taken to the men's side of the tent. A little daughter who would be *her* child. If she lived.

I wanted sons, I thought. But I wanted daughters, too.

In the men's side of the tent, I heard Heber shout, "Does he live?"

I sighed and wiped the tears from my cheeks. Another of the daughters-in-law, a woman my age, handed me a clean, wet cloth, and I wiped my face and hands clean, then went to face Heber.

"The child lives. For now."

"Has he a name?"

"This child is a girl. I don't know if Talliya has yet named her. But the babe is early, and very small and thin; if she lives, it will be a gift of Ya—of the gods," I amended. "Talliya has been sick for so much of the pregnancy—"

He stopped me. "A daughter? That whore has given me a daughter?"

I smiled at him, uncertain. "Your first."

"My last," he said.

I could not believe what I was hearing. "A daughter will care for you in your old age. Will weave and sew and cook, and give you grandchildren—"

"A daughter will not work metal with me. A daughter will not bring trade, or smelt copper, or forge steel. A daughter will be just another useless mouth to feed, and bring me nothing but grief. *No daughters*. I will not have them. Tell the whore that either this child is sacrificed to Baal—for which I will at least get some benefit—or mother and child are to be put aside, and sent away."

CHAPTER
18

We had broken our fast for the day, and the ringing of mallets on metal and the smell of the forging fires filled the camp.

In our tent, all anyone could hear, though, was weeping.

Talliya curled in the corner, nursing her tiny infant and sobbing. Talliya refused to sacrifice her daughter, and since the child was not Heber's firstborn, she had the right to refuse. But it was Heber's right to turn her out, and he had chosen to do this. She would take with her the little boy, who was only four years old, and the baby, barely more than one. And she would take her newborn daughter. And such belongings as she could carry. On Heber's command, she was to be turned out of the camp and into the wilderness before sunset that very night.

We were packing her belongings, trying to figure ways for her to carry those things that could save her life. But how was she to survive? She would not.

She could not, nor could her sweet little boys, nor her tiny, fragile daughter.

Her three older sons were with her, beardless boys reassuring their mother that she would be well, though the youngest wept.

All conversation in the tent stopped when, outside the tent, we heard raised voices—loud and male, and furious.

"You told your concubine . . . *what?*"

In the work yard, all sounds of actual work ceased.

Achaia and I, digging through belongings and trying to salvage only the best for Talliya, stopped what we were doing and exchanged glances.

"You intend to send our mother's sister into the wilderness with a newborn babe? And two small children?"

I recognized that voice as belonging to Zimriqart, Pigat's eldest son.

Heber shouted, "It is my right!"

"It is *my* right to offer her shelter in my tent, then."

"My son thinks he will flout my wishes? I want the useless woman turned out of this camp, where neither she nor her useless young will waste any more of our food. You will honor my wishes—you will abide by my word."

I heard angry muttering, the sounds of men gathering close, voices dropped not because things were growing calmer, but because they were growing more heated.

Talliya cradled her tiny daughter to her breast and opened her eyes. Achaia and I knelt, our hands stilled, our hearts racing, hoping against hope that Heber would relent, that he would come to his senses and honor all that Talliya had done for him in the many years that she had served him with her hands and with her body.

The muttering grew louder and more strained.

And then Zimriqart appeared at our tent and stood, his fists clenched, his face dark with rage. "My honored aunt, beloved sister of my mother—my family will be leaving camp this day, as soon as my wife and sons and daughters and I can pack all we own. You are invited to travel with us, you and your daughter and *all* your beardless sons, as the guest of our household for as long as you live. Blessings be upon you."

That he named her "aunt," and in doing so suggested her status as equal to his mother's, was a thing unthinkable to us all. That he stood for her and against his father in doing so was a hundred times more impossible.

Talliya sat silent for a long moment while tears filled her eyes and then slid down her cheeks. "I am blessed," she said. "I am *blessed*. My thanks to you, son of my sister, blood of my blood, that you have so honored me."

I listened for work to resume, but it did not. So I went around the side of our tent to the outside of the men's side, and saw that Zimriqart was not the only son of Pigat who had walked away from work to begin packing his family.

"You cannot leave me like this!" Heber began shouting. But two of Pigat's other sons were stalking toward their tents, intent on taking their families and their belongings. Packing up everything. Leaving Oak at Zaanannim.

Heber would have the remaining three sons and their sons to help with the work he had been asked by Sisera to do. But I did not see how he and those few men could hope to do everything that had been asked of them.

Zimriqart's wife came to our tent. "We're so sorry to be leaving you here like this," she told me. "I fear things will not go easy on you. I hope when you rejoin us at the main Kenite camp, we'll be able to put all this behind us."

"Heber will never forgive them," I said.

"I hope only that you will forgive us."

"I have nothing to forgive. You are doing only what I would do if I could. I am so grateful that Talliya will be cared for. She is dear to me, my sister and my friend. Keep her safe, and go safely through the wild places. May your footsteps be blessed and your way well-lit until we meet again."

We hugged each other, kissed cheeks, and she said her good-byes to Achaia, too.

Out beneath the tree, we could hear Heber, furious,

roaring at his sons, demanding that those who were staying behind offer no assistance to those who were leaving.

I could only think that he would best serve himself to be silent, perhaps to treat with kindness those who were leaving and to tell them that when he returned to the main Kenite camp all would be forgiven. That they were still his sons.

I thought, if he kept to his current tactics, he was likelier than not to find himself alone in Oak at Zaanannim, with no one but himself to do the smithing, and responsibility for all the repairs for damages that could befall nine hundred chariots in battle, plus the armor for thrice that number for the warriors who would ride in the chariots.

And, as surely as the day follows the night, I heard one of Pigat's sons who would be staying shouting at Heber that he stayed only out of duty to his king— that he and his brothers had drawn lots because *all* of them had wished to escort their mother's sister, Talliya, to safety, but that they understood that they had an obligation, as well, to make sure the work of the king was done in a suitable and honest fashion.

"If you aren't staying out of loyalty to me, begone, all of you," Heber roared.

I closed my eyes.

Silence fell.

Two men stepped into the men's side of the tent, and all of us listened, barely daring to breathe.

"You overstep your common sense and your power, old man," I heard a stranger say. But no, he was not a stranger after all. I dared a quick peek through the flap and saw that he was Sisera's overseer, whose duty it was to make sure the work done for the general—and by extension, for the king—was of suitable quality, and that it was done with the best of materials and in a timely fashion.

Heber stood facing him, shoulders heaving, chin jutted out like a bull's. "I discipline faithless sons, and you declare that I have stepped beyond my authority?"

"You work against the best interests of your king and his general, who will require many hands and many backs to keep their army on its wheels. You cannot do what must be done alone. And if you send these, your sons, away, how do you think that Jabin and Sisera will view what you have done? Will they see it as the work of a loyal and trustworthy ally, do you think?"

The silence from the other side of the tent could have been the silence of the dead.

"Or do you think they will see you as a traitor whose actions have helped their enemy?"

More silence. I could almost have laughed, had I dared. But I was not such a fool as to think that I would not pay a price for laughter.

"I would suggest you apologize to your sons, make amends with them, and forgive them for saving the lives of their aunt and her children. It is a strange thing, is it not, that they value her?" His voice was cutting; it said he found nothing strange about this, that instead he found Heber disgusting. I would never have thought to find in his position someone who agreed with the way I saw Heber.

Heber did trudge off to speak with Pigat's sons who were packing their camps, but none of the three who were leaving could be convinced to stay. All insisted that the journey across the wilderness and back to the Kenite camp would be dangerous—which of course it would—and that they dared not travel with fewer men; strong arms and sturdy blades could mean the difference between survival and death in the bleak spaces between the huddled areas where civilization held the beasts, both two-legged and four-legged, away.

Heber brought Zimriqart into his tent and plied him with wine and dates and figs and bread with olive oil, and told him that he, Heber, would take back Talliya as his concubine if it would bring peace between him and these his sons. He would carry her as his burden, and her daughter, as well.

Achaia and I listened to this conversation alone, because by that time, of course, Talliya had moved all her belongings and joined Zimriqart's household.

We smiled at each other and shook our heads. If he cut either of us loose, nothing in the whole of the world could move us to return to him.

Nor, we quickly discovered, were we alone in this. "You cast Talliya out," Zimriqart said when he had heard the whole of Heber's offer. "You sent her on her way, giving up your claim to her and to her offspring when you did." I could hear the anger in Zimriqart's voice, though he controlled it admirably. None of Heber's sons had his temper; I thought this proved as clearly as anything that they were not his sons. But Heber had never noticed it. Zimriqart said, "My mother's sister made it clear to me before I came here that she has no wish to return to you; that so long as she is welcome in my household, she would wish to live under my roof. Her beardless sons have said the same. They wish to stay with her and work for me."

"They are *my* sons," Heber shouted.

"They are your sons by a concubine, not a wife. You cannot claim their loyalty any more than they can claim an inheritance. They have every right to stay with their mother."

"This dilemma has a simple solution," Heber said. "Make all of them unwelcome under your roof. Talliya can return to mine, with all her sons . . . and even that daughter. Everything will be as it was, you need not have your household inconvenienced—"

And Zimriqart laughed, loudly and long, drowning out anything else that Heber might have had to say. "Inconvenienced? The sister of my mother, who rocked me on her knee and told me stories and cooked me meals when I was a child, will never be an inconvenience to me. Nor will her sons, nor her daughter."

This was not what Heber wanted to hear, but he was mindful of what Sisera's overseer had said to him. This incident could cost him the patronage of Sisera, he seemed finally to realize.

And so he did what I did not think him capable of doing. He said, "Then, if it will mean peace between you and me, my son, I will forgive you taking the woman into your care against my wishes, and grant her and hers my permission to live within this camp while we all are here. So that you need not face the dangers of the wilderness underarmed."

Unmentioned was the fact that these were the same dangers he had expected a mother, a newborn, and two small children to face alone.

"I will speak with my brothers," Zimriqart said after a moment of consideration. "We will sit, we will eat, we will talk together, and I will tell them what you have offered. To do this, we will stay this night within the camp, with your permission, although I cannot promise we will stay tomorrow."

"You are welcome here, my son," Heber said.

I could feel his anger—unspoken, bitten back, chained and bound and waiting. I would, no doubt, feel it much more personally that night. Though I had pitied her and grieved for her when first Heber made his decree, in that moment I envied Talliya for being cast out. She had been set free.

My night was as bad as I could have dreaded.

CHAPTER
19

My next morning held good news, though. Heber's other sons would also stay within the camp. And though Achaia and I were now alone in the tent with Heber, who no longer had a single son living beneath its expanse with him, we could know that Talliya was safe, and we could see her. From time to time we would be able to talk with her. We would not wonder how she and the little one fared; we would not dream at night that they lay in the rough lands, their bones picked by scavengers.

While I was getting this glad news from Ahm-Amat, Sisera's men received word that they were needed to pursue bandits—not Israelites this time, but a band of raiders who had been living in the wilderness and wreaking havoc in towns and villages all around. They tore out of camp in clouds of dust and the accompanying thunder of hooves, and for a while, the whole of the camp seemed quiet.

But I was quick to sense the new order. Heber still

claimed the position of patriarch, but it had become an empty claim. His sons wielded the authority that Heber had always taken for granted, because, to a one, they had made it clear to him they would go back to the Kenite camp and leave him to deal with Sisera and the consequences of his actions, should he act in a fashion they did not like toward Talliya or her offspring.

Heber became an angrier man than I had ever seen him before. He dared not take his anger out on his sons or on his grandsons. He could not take it out on their wives and daughters, for those avoided him at every turn.

He had left only Achaia and me upon which to release his fury.

But even that his sons quickly took away from him. I heard one of them talking to him in quiet tones behind the great oak, as I was drawing water. That son—and I had not seen his face and so did not know which of Pigat's boys he was—said, "We will not stay here and watch you beat them, Heber."

"Beat—who?"

"Your wife. Your concubine."

"You're daring now to tell me how I should treat those who belong to me?"

"No. Of course not. I'm merely telling you that we spoke together this morning, after we heard you blaming your wife last night for all the ills in your life, and after one of our women saw the bruises she bears today. We have decided we will leave if you hurt them again."

"All of you have decided this, have you?"

"Yes. They serve you faithfully. They are patient and obedient. And you treat the camp dogs better than you treat the two of them."

Heber clearly had no intention of accepting the blame for the way he treated us. "Has either of them given me a son? No. Has either of them, then, served me as I am to be served? As the gods themselves have decreed that I am to be served? No. They deserve nothing better than the treatment they receive."

"We do not care in any fashion for your reasons. The jackal has his reasons for killing the goat's kid, doesn't he? Yet we do not give him our sympathy. This we have decided, and I was chosen to come and tell you, for you know that I have served you well all my life, and you know that I am your faithful son."

Heber started to say something else. From my hidden listening post, I could hear him take a deep breath, and say, "Then—"

But Pigat's son did not let him finish. "We have decided, Father. We honor you as our father, but we honor our mother who is gone to Mot, as well. And these, her sister-wife and her sister-concubine, we honor as part of her. Should you treat either of them again as you have treated our aunt, all of us—sons and grandsons alike—will pack our tents and take our wives and our families back to the main camp.

We cannot tell you how to treat them. We can only tell you that we will not stand by to watch as you do it."

I leaned against the cool, rough bark of the tree, breathing hard.

This would infuriate Heber. But I thought it would also keep him from doing that which he would most desire to do—beat us both until neither of us ever moved again.

Because he could not do as King Jabin and Sisera had requested if he was all alone. He could not maintain their weapons and their war chariots and their armor. As one man, he would be helpless. And he would be shamed, for what sort of father would he be if all his sons and grandsons were willing to pack up and leave him? To abandon him?

While he needed them, I thought, Achaia and I would be safe enough.

I did not dare to think how our lives would change once he was free to return to the main Kenite camp. When he could work with other smiths rather than his own sons, I did not think our lives would be worth a bowl of burned wheat.

At the edge of the camp, at that moment, I heard a woman scream, and then the shout of men's voices and the clang of swords.

Both Heber and his son raced toward the sound of the trouble.

I hauled my water back to our tent as quickly as I could and grabbed Achaia—both of us ran to the center of the camp, to the tent of Zimriqart, which was nearest the well. The other women were grabbing children and babies and pulling them into that tent—Achaia and I, with no children of our own, looked for our sisters who were not yet safe and ran to their tents to help them bring in their little ones. There were so many. Heber might be a dried stalk, but his sons were not. They had sons, and their sons had sons and daughters—though many more boys than girls—so that during the daytime camp overflowed with the high voices of little ones.

We carried children to the safer center of the camp and ran back to the edges in search of more—and always in the background we could hear men fighting, men shouting, swords and mallets swinging, and the screams of the wounded, and the horrible sobs of the dying.

We huddled together, but I realized that if all of us hid within the tent, those most in need of protection—the mothers with babies and small children, would have no defense if the bandits broke through. One of Heber's grandsons recognized it at the same time. He was perhaps five years younger than I—still too small and weak to take up arms where the fighting was fiercest, but old enough to stand at the tent flap. He looked around at the rest

169

of us, clearly frightened, but he picked up one of the tent mallets and walked to the flap, where he took up watch.

I rose and grabbed another mallet, and went to stand beside him. I was childless. I could fight, I thought.

Achaia rose next—but she did not take a mallet. Instead, she armed herself with two sharpened tent pegs.

The older boys and the older girls and the few other very young wives who were without children or who were not yet visibly with child rose, and they armed themselves with whatever they could find.

We held in our hands tent mallets and pegs. Some of our number found weapons among the smiths' working tools—awls, hammers, pry bars.

If the men could not hold the line, then we would be the last stand. We who did not have children would do what we could to protect those who did.

I was afraid. I had never been so afraid in my life. Not even Heber did I fear as much as I feared the men who dared attack us in the early morning, who were jackals so bold that they thought they could take on a camp of men who worked metal for gain—strong, hard men—and conquer them.

I wondered who those jackals were. What they wanted. Who had sent them. I wondered if they would reach us, break through our thin line—I wondered how we might suffer in their hands. I wondered if we could hold them back.

The mallet in my hand was heavy, carved of a hardwood that felt almost like stone. I held its handle, swinging it slowly back and forth, getting the feel of it, trying to imagine striking a man with it. I stared outward, praying that I would not face the moment when I had to do that very thing, or die.

From beyond the outer ring of tents I could still hear the shouting and the fighting, but less. The screaming as well, also diminished.

The dying. Yes. The dying, too.

Soon, men would move into the inner ring of the tents, and either they would be our men, coming to tell us that they had won the day, or they would be our enemies, coming to claim their spoils.

Those spoils would be us. The women. The children. The babies. Everything we owned.

I found myself wishing that Sisera and his men had not been off chasing bandits, though I had been glad enough to see them go when they were called away. They would have stood side to side with our men. They would have fought.

But then I realized that whoever attacked us had been watching the camp, waiting for them to leave. We were probably being attacked by the bandits they were hunting—by men who were sure they could not fight off trained warriors, but who thought the men left behind would be vulnerable, either to their numbers or to their arms. Or perhaps to both.

I held the mallet tighter, with my heart racing and the palms of my hands sweating. I licked my lips and looked over at one of Heber's granddaughters, not much younger than I, who held sharpened tent pegs in each hand. She was wide-eyed with terror, but she did not run inside the tent to hide with the mothers and babies.

The boys, young and thin, wore fierce expressions on their faces, certain that they could fight off these bandits who came with swords and spears, and bows and arrows. I could see no doubt in their eyes.

I envied them. If I died, I wished I would be able to do it without being consumed by doubt.

And then the last of the crashing and the clanging fell to silence. A cry went up. A cheer.

But whose cheer?

Now it comes, I thought.

Either our people, or our enemies.

I raised the mallet and tensed, ready to fight. Around the tent, the other young wives, the other older children, the few concubines, did the same.

We no longer gave each other glances. Now we stared ahead, watching, waiting.

And the first men to step into view were so bloody, so dirt-caked and mired that I did not know if they were theirs our ours.

They stopped, staring at us, and then one of them

shouted, "Jael! Hurry, help us. We have injured men among us—your husbands and fathers. Be quick."

The mallet dropped from my fingers, and suddenly I shook so hard, my knees gave way, and I found myself sitting in the dirt. The young wives began to weep, the little girls to sob—I even saw lips trembling on the little boys. I dragged myself to my feet, though, and ran forward with the others, and we began making places within the nearest tents to treat our injured. Beyond the edge of the camp, our men quickly finished off the enemy wounded and debated setting off after the few survivors who had retreated.

Instead, they decided to send up a pillar of smoke to draw back Sisera and his men. They would surely return to see what was causing that.

I helped clean and bandage wounds, not seeing Heber, hoping that he was one of the men we had lost.

If he were dead, I would be a widow. If he were dead, I could be free. Poor, with no place to go, perhaps.

But he would no longer hurt me, or frighten me. I would never have to fear him again.

When at last Heber appeared, only scratched, still alive, I did what I could to hide my disappointment, and greeted him as the other wives greeted their husbands.

As if I were happy to see him.

CHAPTER
20

We mourned the dead, and that same day burned their bodies on pyres. Fathers and sons we bade good-bye, husbands and children. Five of our own we lost in the fighting, but our losses were not so steep as those of the bandits. A dozen of their bodies the uninjured men rolled down the nearest ravine, to be food for the beasts. They wiped their shoes on those men.

Back in the camp, we fought to save the living. Sisera and his men went out across the plains and hunted down the survivors of the bandits, desperate men who had been raiding small towns and caravans and tent camps like ours for some time, stealing food, camp goods, tents, anything and anyone they might hope to sell. They killed anyone who had no value to them—the old, or dangerous, or pregnant, or children.

They had been a scourge in the area, and even then, neither Sisera nor his men knew where they

hid. Our men knew there had been survivors. They
loosed some of the camp dogs and followed them,
hoping to track the monsters to their hiding place,
but they failed.

There were not many bandits who'd survived,
though. They would be less bold.

But we had little time to think about them. We
women had the nursing of the wounded to attend
to, along with the cooking and the tending of children, the spinning and sewing and washing. For
those of us without children who could be put to
those tasks, we also had fuel-gathering and goat-
tending and milking and halab-making. The men had
to work doubly hard, for with the dead gone and the
injured recuperating, they still had to meet the needs
of Sisera's army.

Heber spoke neither to Achaia nor to me. This I
considered a blessing; she did, as well. He ate alone,
drank alone, slept alone.

I thought if I could be married to him in that fashion for the rest of my life, it would not be such a
bad thing.

But of course, after this battle, we would leave Oak
at Zaanannim, and return to the life we had known
with him before. That life I didn't want back at all.

Three days after the bandit attack, Achaia was
mending one of Heber's kuttonets when she stopped,
lifted her head, and froze.

"What?" I asked her.

"Listen," she said.

I listened. I could hear brass bells blowing in the wind, and the sounds of wagons creaking to a halt, the clack and clatter of wagon wheels, the patient sighing of oxen and asses.

"Caravan," I whispered, putting aside my weaving shuttle and loom, and smiling.

"Caravan," she agreed. "But how our situation has changed since last we bought from a caravan." She glanced to the corner where her mattress lay rolled, and to the broken pot bottom tucked partially under it. "We'll not need to buy much this time, with just the three of us here," she said.

"Need? This isn't about need. This is about us getting the only good thing we can out of being married to Heber. Well . . . of *me* being married to Heber. We're going to buy every wonderful thing in the caravan, Achaia. Heber has the trade of the king of Hazor and his whole army—he is wealthier than either you or I could imagine. And we are going to show people his wealth. First, we're going to buy new pots so that when we return to the Kenite camp, we can give back all that we borrowed. Next, we're going to obtain enough wheat to feed an army, because neither of us is ever going to be beaten because we had to make a meal of barley again. And other foods, too, for is Heber's tent not a stopping place for generals and soldiers?" I glared at the cloth wall that separated us from the other half of the tent.

"Those are reasonable things."

"They are," I agreed. "But this isn't about being reasonable," I said, and my voice turned grim. "When we've finished buying all that is reasonable and sensible, we'll get pretty cloth, fine perfume, spinning wool, dyestuffs, dyed rovings, jewelry, hair combs and pins. Glass beads, maybe mirrors. Not only do we have to feed Heber's guests; when we serve their food we have to present the image that he is a successful man, rich and powerful. It is part of our duty, and it's a duty we cannot carry out without spending some of his wealth."

If I could have, I would have found a way to spend it all. I would have impoverished him. I would have left him destitute, because even though I would still be married to him while he was destitute, I would be able to see that he got what he deserved.

Thus I would have had my revenge before he accused me of keeping myself from having a child and threw me to the priests, who would see that I died.

"You could get rings and bracelets," Achaia told me. "Gold and turquoise and lapis lazuli and silver for your hair. I don't think I should get anything, though. Perhaps some more wool to spin. I'm not his wife."

We left our cooking and weaving, and hurried to the caravan with the other wives and daughters. The men were working, and would have to visit in the twilight when the workday was done.

We bought our wheat first, a ridiculous amount—but I had decided my shame over the barley would never be repeated. After that, we went to the stall where we could select replacement pots.

And the same trader from whom we had bought Achaia's father's pot was in that stall. He recognized us.

As we began pointing out cook pots that we wanted, he moved close to Achaia and said, "I have . . . news. Sent from your family. They know where you are, and that you are well. They have survived, and Yahweh willing, they will find a way to bring you home. Be ready, be vigilant, and have faith."

He backed away, and marked the pots we had chosen. We moved on, doing our best to act as we always did—we did not want to draw attention to ourselves, or cause suspicion.

But I could no longer look at wool, or at jewelry, or at any of the lovely things I had thought to buy. I could only think that Levi of Kadesh had done as I had asked him. He had gotten word home. He had not forgotten us when he left the camp with his sword. He had honored his promise, and in doing so acknowledged the value of Achaia's life.

I could see his face. His smile. I could hear his voice and imagine his kindness as he walked beside me, and as he pulled the water out of the well for me.

I had to stop and turn my face away from Achaia for a moment to fight back my tears. All I had ever wanted was to be what my mother was: a good and faithful helpmeet, a wife who stood at her husband's side and cared for him as he cared for her, and who raised their children to honor him, to honor her, and to be people both her husband and she could be proud of. Had that been so much to want? My parents could not have known about Heber—he had offered well for me, and they had believed that meant he would value me. To them, for whom such an offering would have required a lifetime of saving and scraping, the great worth of Heber's offering had been a demonstration of the great value he would place on me. They were simple people who had never been rich, and they would not understand that to a man who could own whatever he wanted, no sacrifice had been involved in his offering for me.

It had been something to toss at the people who had what he wanted. And when he got me, he found out I wasn't what he wanted after all.

I would give up everything, I thought, to have a marriage like the one my parents had.

If only such a thing were possible.

I got myself under control and realized that Achaia was speaking to me, and I had not heard a single word she said.

"What?" I asked her.

"I was wondering if you had considered what I might do to stay ready. The man told me I was to be vigilant."

"We'll consider the steps we should take. Everyone is making ready to go to war—it will be only a few more days. If your people come here to take you back, we should make sure that your belongings are in one place. Perhaps in a bag, so that you can catch hold of it as you run."

"What if they don't come into the camp, though? What if they're expecting me to run to them?"

"I wish the man had said more," I told her. Her problems, at least, could keep my mind off my own. When she was gone, when she was on her way back to her people and her life, I would be alone with Heber.

That didn't bear thinking about.

So when we made our way back to our tent, we did not go visiting. We sat on the carpet with our heads together, talking in low voices.

Our hands stayed busy with the mending, but our words were not of homelike things.

"If you must run, you'll need water," I said, "and a bit of food. We'll need a water skin for you, and cloth in which to wrap dried figs, and some lehem."

"I should not take much with me if I have to run. I don't want to be accused of stealing if I get caught. If I have a big bag with me, I surely will."

I thought about that. She was right, and thieves

faced penalties as brutal as adulteresses. We could not allow her to look as if she were robbing Heber.

"Then we'll have a little bag for you to take if you have to run after them, and a big one we can hand to you if they come to get you."

She nodded. "That seems sensible. Only—how will I know until it's too late that I was supposed to go after them?"

I pondered that. "Either they'll find a way to get word to you, or else they'll come for you. It's the only way that they could hope you would know what to do."

She nodded. And then she looked at me with eyes dark with worry and sharp with discernment. "And when I am gone, what will become of you, my sister? How will you fare in Heber's tent when you and he are alone inside it?"

That, of course, was the question about which I had no desire to think. The future lay before me like an abyss.

I did not know what I would do. I knew only all the things that I wished that I could do, and that I could not, because I was bound to Heber, and I had only two ways out of that. The first was a divorce that only he could choose—and that would leave me homeless and destitute, shamed among my people, seen as worthless, fit for nothing but to sit at the gate with my face veiled, while I offered myself to strangers.

The second was death.

I was determined to be free of Heber, though. In my heart, I prayed to Yahweh-Shalom that he could see a third path that I could not.

Achaia, watching my face, said, "I cannot bear to think of you left behind with him. I will stay with you, so that you do not have to face him alone."

"You cannot. Go back to your own people, and live a good life. We follow the paths we are given, and this is mine. We will bear what we must. We are women, after all."

Then I thought of a ludicrous idea, but it filled me with hope. "When you are with them, beg them to take me, too. Tell them that I will gladly be a slave, that I will not fight or flee if they come to take me. Better a slave in a stranger's house than being the right wife of rich Heber."

And Achaia nodded. Neither of us saw anything strange about that choice.

I dreamed that night of fleeing Heber—of setting off across the wilderness with Achaia as my companion. But bears attacked us, and lions, and jackals. Vultures flew over us, and in the end, the two of us were nothing but bones. I could see our bones scattered, gleaming on the rocky ground, almost as if they had been polished.

I considered myself warned: if we stayed where we were, we might die, but if we fled, we surely would.

So I would pray, then, that Heber's enemies would come to our rescue.

CHAPTER

21

We came at last to the day before the battle.
Achaia had received no further word, so we
had packed a large bag for her and put the smaller
one aside, just in case word came at the last moment.

That day, we cooked for much of the army, and I
did not even have the time to gloat over the stores I
had laid in that made this possible.

Every woman in the camp was doing as we were:
cooking. Sisera came to the tent and sat awhile with
Heber, but he had not the time to stay and feast; he
was taking his men into the field of battle, and his
attention was on matters of war.

We kept to the background, Achaia and I. Carried
cook pots full of steaming nazim and baskets of
bread and nebels of wine, and kept our heads down
and our faces hidden as best we could.

We wanted no notice from men boisterous before
a battle, men who were not of our people, and who
might not care that we were married. Adultery was

a woman's sin to my people, and we would die all the same, whether we sought out the attentions of men or had their attentions forced upon us.

Better we remained as shadows.

We watched the gleaming chariots rolling away, the long last rays of the setting sun burnishing them gold and glinting and glittering off the scaled iron. When the last of the warriors rolled out of sight, and the thundering of horses' hooves died away, I found myself still watching the column of dust that rose in their wake.

They rode toward Mount Tabor, and to the broad plain by the Kishon River in the Jezreel Valley, where the armies would meet. The dust from Canaanite wheels and the horses' hooves rose up, marking their location to any who cared to see it. They were the mighty army of Sisera, with the strength of nine hundred chariots, with archers and swordsmen, with thousands of horses. In all the world, whom did they have to fear?

I was glad to see them go.

Whatever happened now would happen.

"We travel in the hands of Yahweh," Achaia told me, resting her own hand on my shoulder.

I could only nod my agreement. "On the morrow, your new life should begin." I sighed. "And mine."

We turned away from the cloud of dust—all that remained of the mighty spectacle that had been so much a part of our lives these last months.

Behind us, the men of our camp cheered. They

gathered in the center of our camp, dancing and drinking wine. The women took the small children and retreated into the tents, dropping the walls, and pegging them into place to make a safe space against the fall of night.

A huge job was done, and what would follow would be a night of drunken revelry—men with strong wine in plenty, and time at last to catch their breath after the unending work of the last months. I could not blame them for their happiness, but I knew full well I wanted to stay out of their way.

The meal we made for Heber sat in his side of the tent, the pots covered and waiting, but he did not come for it. We ate a little, for we had been cooking all day, and had not had time to feed ourselves. And then, with darkness fallen and the noise of the men singing and dancing and drinking, telling loud tales and making big brags, throwing bones and wagering in the tent corners, I lay down to sleep.

I awoke to the sound of screaming.

"You were praying!"

The sound of flesh hitting flesh, and a scream.

I sat up, clutching the wool blanket that covered me.

"You were praying to that Israelite god of yours. You have brought evil into my house." Another hard hit, another scream. I shuddered, and not realizing what I was doing, found myself on my feet and at the flap between Heber's side of the tent and ours.

185

"You've been cursing us, you witch. Cursing me and my family. My first wife is dead because of you, my second wife is barren, the concubine who gave me sons gave birth to a daughter, and then emptied my tent so that I am alone. With you."

"No," Achaia wailed. "I never prayed for curses. I prayed only for good things. That I could go home. That I could see my mama and my sisters again. Never any harm to you or yours."

I'd already figured out what was going on. Heber came into our side of the tent, certainly drunk and probably looking to take one of us into his bed for the night, and had discovered me asleep and Achaia in prayer to Yahweh-Shalom. In his mind, he had seen her prayers as the secret cause of all his ills. He would never see his own behavior as bringing down misery upon his head.

He hit her again, and I stepped through the flap into his side. He had her by the hair, lifted in front of him, her feet barely touching the ground. I did not think she would be able to stand if he released her. Her mouth bled, and her nose. Her jaw curved at an odd angle. Her eyes were open, but they stared at nothing. She no longer wept or cried out. Her face hung slack.

"Get out of here," he snarled at me. "This witch is the reason you're barren. She's been cursing us."

You've killed her, I thought. *She's dead.* "She isn't," I said. "She hadn't done anything wrong."

I'd not thought it possible for his face to look any

angrier, but in that instant, I discovered I was wrong. "I *caught* her!" he said. "I caught her cursing us, praying to her god that is the enemy of our gods! I caught her!"

Terrified of him, of his anger and what he could do to me, I still reached out a hand to him. "Husband of mine, she has no evil in her. She is only a girl who wanted to go home. Let her go, that your sons and your grandsons do not desert you and leave us here in this place alone. If they do, we will be nothing but pickings for vultures within days."

He lowered his arms, and Achaia sagged bonelessly to the floor, her eyes half-open. She breathed— I could see as he lowered her to the ground that she still breathed, and it seemed that once again I could breathe, as well. I could only hope that she did not move or make a noise in hopes of avoiding his further anger.

"You knew of that?" he asked me, and his voice was suddenly even, and soft.

"I . . . heard," I said. "Word at the well, no doubt passed and changed from mouth to mouth. But still, yes. I knew."

He nodded. He looked down a slumped and silent Achaia, and said, "Yes. You would hear. Women talk about everything, don't they? Sooner or later, the word reaches the well and all secrets are as nothing. A man has no privacy if his women gather water at the well."

He sounded bitter, but quietly bitter.

He released Achaia's hair and turned away, his shoulders slumped.

"I'll not lose my sons. Tomorrow we can take her out and stone her. But tonight, I'll not touch her again. I'll have my sons know her for the witch that she is, and take such measures as they must against the woman who brought death to their mother. Tomorrow, we'll decide this thing as it should be decided."

He staggered over to his mat with the wide stance of the drunken, and fell onto it. His eyes closed, his mouth fell open, and within an instant he was asleep.

I turned my attention to Achaia.

She had not moved from the spot where he'd dropped her.

I knelt beside her and touched her shoulder. "Achaia?"

She did not respond to my voice, or to my touch.

She breathed. She still bled from her mouth, a thin trickle that slid down one corner, while from her nose, a steady, slow stream ran.

Her eyes already bore the shadows that would be dark bruises on the morrow. Her lips were split, her jaw displaced.

I could see nothing, though, that might have taken the sense from her. He must have hit her head. That would sometimes leave someone senseless, even if there was no visible injury.

I realized that the last time he hit her, she had not screamed.

I crouched before her and wrapped her arms around my shoulders as if I were putting on a cloak, and stood, leaning forward enough to balance her weight on my hips and back. She was as slender as I; she was not terribly hard to move.

I got her over to our side of the tent, put her on her mattress, and tried to wake her by splashing cool water on her face, but it didn't work. I looked into her eyes, which still were closed only partway. They stared straight forward, seeing nothing. Sometimes they blinked. But they did not move to focus on me when I leaned over her, nor did they follow me as I moved away.

He had done something very bad to her. I could feel it in my belly, and in the way the hairs rose up on my arms and on the back of my neck. I could feel that this was not some tiny thing that would pass, and leave her awake and talking to me in the morning.

I could not see the place where Achaia's hurt lay, but I knew whatever Heber had done to her was more than I could fix with my little knowledge of childbirthing and the few herbs my mother had taught me to boil for fevers and loose bowels.

Gentle manipulation put her jaw back into place— I heard the click and saw her face return to its former shape. It was a blessing, I supposed, that she had not been awake for that.

But I had no idea what to do next. We had older women in the camp with more experience in healing than I had. I needed their hands and their wisdom.

As a practical matter, I turned Achaia to her side. When we had cared for my great-grandfather in his last days, he had become quite sick. My mother had trained me never to leave him on his back when he was to be alone, because if he vomited, he would drown. The things we learn from the care of our elders we are wise to apply to the care of the young, too. I minded my mother's teaching, and when I was sure Achaia was as safe as I could make her, ran for help.

Latiya, Zimriqart's wife, was first to arrive. She crouched by Achaia's side and rested two fingers on the pulse of her throat. "Her heart beats strong and steady, but quick as a bird's," she said.

I nodded. "Her eyes open and close, but when you say her name, nothing changes. She doesn't look, she doesn't answer. It's as if she has gone away and left her still-living body behind.

Several other wives crowded into the tent, and the flickering of the lanterns they'd carried brightened the space. Each in turn knelt beside Achaia; all agreed that they knew of nothing they might do to help her. She was beyond them. Beyond all of us. She was in the hands of the gods, they said.

In the hands of Yahweh-Shalom, I thought.

They tied colored cords around her wrist—green for health and strength, and blue for healing. They whispered their chants to Asherah and rocked back and forth. A few at a time I gave the story of what had happened to her, carefully edited to make it sound as though she had been faithfully praying at the altars of the gods. I passed off what had happened as Heber's drunken misinterpretation of what he had seen—and since everyone knew Heber and his rages and his willingness to lay blame anywhere but as his own feet, they accepted my affirmation that she was not a witch who had been cursing us.

Several of them apparently knew the truth of Heber's situation, as well, for when I mentioned that Heber said Achaia had cursed me with barrenness, they had started softly laughing.

"The gods themselves cursed Heber," Latiya whispered to me. "For having the intelligence of the stupidest sheep and the temper of the worst mule."

"Will all of you leave now, though?" I asked her. "If you do, it will leave me here alone with Achaia and Heber. And no one to help either of us."

Latiya frowned. "I don't know what my husband and his brothers, or the rest of the men, will wish to do. I cannot imagine them leaving the three of you here, if their wish was to preserve you from his temper. But they cannot take you with them; you are Heber's wife. Nor can they take Achaia—for all that she does not move or speak, still she is his property, and the man among them who stepped in to take her away would be a thief.''

I nodded.

The truth was rarely a pleasant thing. Necessary, but not pleasant. If she still breathed, help for Achaia might come with the morning light and the battle that would begin then. She would not be able to speak for me, though, to offer me as a slave in exchange for my escape from Heber. There was no help for me, unless it came direct from Yahweh's hand.

CHAPTER

22

I did not sleep much during the night. One of the women tending Achaia bade me lie down for a rest, and I closed my eyes, but when I did, I could not find the silence of sleep. Instead, all I saw was Heber, with Achaia held by her hair in one of his big hands, screaming at her and hitting her and shaking her like a camp dog with a rat.

When I did drift into sleep, nightmares plagued me: Heber pursued as I ran; spears came at me from all directions; I found myself in Hazor again, close to my parents' house. But when I ran to their door and pounded on it, begging them to help me, Heber answered. I was in the square, and men surrounded me with stones in their hands, and I begged them not to kill me.

I woke. Waking was better than sleeping; being free of the chains my dreams wound around me made even grim reality and my present situation look better.

No one, after all, was trying to stone me. That, to me, seemed a good thing.

I only prayed the dream held no prophecy in it, for I could not consider myself safe from Heber's threat to accuse me of using secret means to rid myself of pregnancy.

Dawn came at last, and we began the chores of the day. Now it was only me, for the women who could stay to tend to Achaia could not distract themselves with cooking and drawing and carrying water and carrying fuel and tending the fire and grinding the grain.

I did what I could, but I made no effort to create any sort of lovely meal for Heber. He got wheat, parched, and unleavened bread, and dried figs because we had them in plenty, and a bowl of fresh goat's milk, not curdled, because I did not have the time or the temper to take effort for him.

He held his head as if it pained him, and I found myself wishing that it would split in twain, as if cleaved by some warrior's sword. I found myself wishing him dead, and horribly dead at that, with much pain and shame and suffering going before it.

But much as I wanted to pray for his death, I did not. I prayed only for my own freedom, even if it might be in death. And for Achaia to be released from Heber's cruelty, as well.

I could not know that her Yahweh-Shalom would listen to me anymore, since she could no longer speak to him. I could not guess if he would hear me without her.

But I didn't know if he'd been listening since I started praying to him, either. I could only believe.

The men went about their chores. They were starting their forges for the day—they had some work they could do, but they were primarily waiting for the battle to start, and for the first of the damaged vehicles, pieces of armor, and swords to be brought in. The men who brought them would probably not be able to return to battle in the same day. But they might be able to stop fleeing enemies or take them captive.

It should not be much of a day for the men, though. We all knew this. Their part of the war was mostly done before it began—and wouldn't intensify again until it was well and truly over.

I could hear the chariots rolling, the thunder of the horses' hooves. Sometimes, I could hear the shouts of the men, as well.

The battle had started, the war was upon us, and soon Achaia's salvation would be at hand—if any hope for her existed anymore—or she and I would be doomed to face our fate at Heber's hands.

The sounds died away. I took my turn at tending Achaia, talking to her, turning her from side to side so that she would not get sores on her skin, washing her and cleaning her.

She could not swallow water. We had tried her on

195

it, sitting her up, leaning her forward, carefully giving her the smallest of sips. We ended up turning her on her side and letting it run back out again.

If she could not take water, she could not take food, and without food or water, she would soon be dead.

I urged her to wake up. I did not know if she could hear me, but I prayed that she could.

"Today is the day," I told her. "Today they'll come for you, to take you back to your family. Your mother is waiting for you," I whispered. "She believes you well, and if she cannot see you smile at her when the brave soldiers take you back to her, her heart will break. You must wake up."

She did not. I held her hand, mopped her brow, turned her, talked to her, and all the while knew that not far away, a fate we could not guess at was being decided for us, with men's arms and men's swords and men's courage.

Either her rescue would come, or it would not.

And then I heard a rumble, and thought at first that it must be drums. Sisera and his men had drummers and tambourine players who sometimes accompanied them into battle. I did not know what the Israelites used—I had never before been close enough to where the battle would be fought to hear the sounds of it.

Then, however, I looked out of the opened walls of the tent and saw that the clear sky was darkening.

I frowned. The rains should not come for another two months. I stared at the sky, watching clouds pulling closer together, growing larger, growing darker. Lightning flashed not far away, and after a moment the thunder roared in my ears and shook the ground.

One of Heber's grandsons, who with the other older boys was watching the battle from high ground, came running into camp.

"The Canaanites have the advantage!" he shouted.

This was no surprise to anyone, of course. The Israelites had no chariots, and even if they had brought greater numbers to the fight, they would have been at a disadvantage.

The men, though, gathered round to hear the news. I could hear it well enough through the tent wall, and satisfied myself with sitting at Achaia's side, watching her breathe, and listening to the men's voices.

"The Israelites have a sturdy host of archers," the boy was saying. "And swordsmen and pikemen in plenty. But they have nothing to move them about."

Thunder drowned out his next words.

"Have they met in battle yet?"

"Not yet," the boy said. "I was sent to give the news of the disposition of the armies. They were heading toward each other across the plains, but the Israelites are still clinging to the edges of the highland, as if they plan to retreat."

Ann Burton

"Will they turn and run, do you think?" one of the men asked the other.

"I don't think so. They've been skirmishing and testing at the outskirts of the Canaanite forces. I think this time they have as many men as they're likely to get, and that they'll engage."

"You think they have any chance of winning?" the same man asked.

And the same respondent answered. "Of course not. Men on foot against iron chariots, fast horses, and—"

The next crack of thunder shook the ground beneath us. I jumped, and rose to peek out of the tent.

The men were staring up at the sky, which had turned black and angry.

"It won't come to anything," Heber said. "It never does this time of year."

"Looks like something," one of his sons said. "Looks like it could be a great deal of something."

I stared up at the clouds. They had that bulging, pregnant look the sky gets when it is filled with rain. I looked at the few scattered drops still falling, big and loose and heavy, and I thought the sky would soon open up.

I left Achaia long enough to put the side walls down on Heber's side of the tent. I did not want to have Heber angry with me for letting the rain soak his belongings; I had enough other worries that day. If heavy rains came, the tent would drip a bit no matter what I did, but unless it turned into a days-long deluge, we would stay dry enough. Then I closed the walls on our side and staked them into place.

I went back to Achaia's side. She hadn't changed. She breathed; her eyes were closed; she didn't move.

In my heart, I felt an assurance that my prayers had been heard. That Achaia would be rescued, and that she would be well again. I could see no evidence to support this, though. The Canaanites were set to win the war, and if they won, Achaia would get no rescue from the Israelites.

This was our reality—we were two women in a place where women were of little value beyond what they could produce—and we, who could not produce what was wanted of us, had become disposable. We existed at Heber's humor, which was none too good.

But even focusing on what I knew to be true, I could not help but feel a faint elation. The two of us were not alone. Yahweh-Shalom worked in our favor, hidden from all eyes.

Then came more news—another of the young boys from the high ground.

"The armies have met at the edges, and the Canaan-ites win their contests with the blade. The bowmen of both sides hold the fight at some distance yet, but the Canaanites have run the Israelites toward the Kishon River, and when they reach it, they shall not be able to pass.

CHAPTER

23

So it was that my faint hope and my unseemly elation were dashed upon the ground. The Canaanites won their battles, even if the armies were not fully engaged, even if the Israelites hung back.

Sisera would hold the day, as he had held the many days that had preceded it.

The others had gone some time ago, after assuring themselves that Achaia's condition had not changed. I sat in the tent—twilight-dark at midday—without any idea what I should do. I stroked Achaia's hair and whispered to her, "If they will not come for us, we will find a way to go to them. Only wake up. Only open your eyes, and you and I shall flee this place, no matter the consequences. Just wake up."

But she did not. She lay insensible as the moment she had fallen.

Latiya, Zimriqart's wife, returned from her household to sit with me.

"I brought wool, spindle, and distaff," she said. "I thought you might like to have someone with you during your vigil."

"I would," I said. I heard a sudden drumming on the tent roof and looked up. "There it is. The rain. The sky has broken loose."

"And out of season," Latiya said. "How very strange for this to come up out of a clear sky, so suddenly."

The breeze that blew in through the flap smelled of dust and the freshness of water. I inhaled the sudden sweetness of the air. "I'm grateful," I said. "How fresh it feels."

"If it came in season, it would be cold," Latiya said, coming to stand by the tent flap with me.

Outside, the world had turned silver, water sheeting from the sky as if the whole of the sea raced over the edge of heaven to deluge us.

Untimely it fell, and yet it did not fall unwelcome. I did not know why I rejoiced to see rain so hard as this, but still, I did. My heart leapt again to the elation it had known earlier.

The hand of the One God was in this rain, I thought, though I could not think why he would bring rain on this day.

Still.

I turned to Latiya. "Will you watch her for me while I change my clothes?" I asked. "I do not wish to still be wearing this old, threadbare robe when they come to announce the winning of the war. I'll end up making Heber look poor, and he'll be angry."

Latiya said, "Change, certainly. Dear sister, I bring news to you."

I pulled off the old red kuttonet, and rinsed myself with the water I had carried from the well earlier. Then I slipped on the beautiful blue kuttonet that I'd made. I turned briefly to Latiya. "What news do you bring?"

"After the battle, Heber's sons and grandsons will be pulling up stakes and leaving camp. All of us, to a one. When our husbands heard of Achaia's condition, they agreed that we could not stay any longer. So the wives are packing. Some of the husbands, too, in truth."

"Does Heber know yet?" I asked, thinking that this was the sort of news I would hope he'd never get wind of. He would hate me all the more; he would blame me for my sins against him, for turning his family against him, for in some way being involved in Achaia's downfall the night before. He would be furious at me, because I was the only one left to be furious at—and his only other alternative was to take the blame himself. That, I felt sure, he would never do.

"We had thought to not tell him until we began packing outside the tents. We hoped to win ourselves some little space of quiet and peace while we worked, before he charged into our tents, screaming accusations."

"That's what he'll do," I said. I stared over at all our new cook pots. "Hide your pottery first. You don't want to have to replace everything."

"I wish we could take you with us," Latiya said.

"No more than I do. But I'll stay. I have to take care of Achaia, and after that . . ." My words trailed to nothing. I could not imagine any future for myself once everyone else had gone.

Strangers would come to the well, and move on. Perhaps a caravan would pass again, and we would be able to travel with it, with the number of travelers conferring some safety.

But try as I might to see myself in this tent come the next sunrise, or the one after that, I could not bring the image clear. It seemed to me that my life would end this day. That I would not cook another meal within these walls than the one that I was cooking, with the walls in that corner still lifted a bit to permit the smoke to blow out.

The rain fell steadily.

Would this be the day that Heber lost his temper completely with me. That he killed me?

I could believe it. With Achaia senseless and his sons packing their belongings to leave him because of what he'd done to her, I could imagine that he would turn his rage on me, and the full brunt of his fists would be the end of me.

And with no help coming from the war . . .

"Your mind is far away," Latiya said.

"It is. I wonder at the progress of the war, though it has little enough to do with me. My work will be the same no matter who wins."

She nodded. "It is hard not to wonder what is happening on the plains beyond this hill. Hard to sit here spinning and think about men dying in the dirt just beyond the place where we can see."

"Dying." I nodded, and stared at the rug beneath my feet. Red and purple, gold and green, it bore the patterns of birds and flowers and leaves, and in the center, vining spirals that enchanted the eye. Someone had woven it with love, working the complicated designs one thread and one knot at a time, making the vines twist and twine around each other. Who? Who had been the woman or man to sit patiently at the task. Had he or she lived in my lifetime. Did he live still?

I had made nothing like that rug that I would leave behind. I had no great work that someone would sit and admire and wonder at. I had women's work. My weaving, all of it simple. My spinning. My sewing. My cooking. No one would ever touch anything of mine and say, "She was once here." When I died, I would vanish. No child would mourn me; no one would need me.

But I wore my blue kuttonet, and for some reason, it reminded me of Yahweh-Shalom, and the way he lived within the hearts of his worshippers, and the way the blue reflected the sky which was everywhere, and which touched all things as he did.

I got out the jewelry, and from the collection left behind after Talliya moved out, I found the headband that had belonged to Pigat, the one with the five gold almond flowers. I put it on.

And then I painted my eyes with kohl and wove my hair back in a long braid that I left hanging down my back. If I lived—if that were the will of Achaia's god—then I would live bravely, and face whatever came. If I died this day, then I would do it wearing my best clothing, as a woman of substance and means. I would not cower in a corner. I would protect Achaia with everything in me, and protect myself second.

This I promised.

"You look beautiful," Latiya said. "Think you to seduce Heber, and so calm him when he hears the angry news?"

"I could never calm him," I told her. "He wants nothing of me but the child that I cannot give him. He wants me to give him something I cannot. And perhaps it is me, and perhaps it is him—"

She put her finger to my lips. "I know the truth. The helpful priest is back in the main Kenite camp, and nothing you could do would bring forth a baby until you got his . . . blessing."

"I won't," I said.

She looked shocked and sad. "Not ever?"

"I promised I would be faithful to Heber."

"But if you don't give him what he wants, he'll eventually kill you. He'll be sure it's your fault, because his other wife and his concubine gave him children."

"I know." I knelt on the rug with the pretty pattern and sat with my head down, listening to the rain falling, pouring out of the sky as heavy as the sea upended. When I looked up at her, it was to shrug. "I cannot fix one wrong with another wrong. I want babies. I want to be able to know that I have no cause to feel guilty about them, though."

She came and sat beside me. "I understand. How can I not? I have seen how he treats the woman who gave him five sons and a daughter. How would he treat one who gave him a dozen, if he found out they were not of his seed? He would not care for her suffering and hard work, her pain and labor, or that he was called the father. He would care only that she be made to suffer more for her unfaithfulness."

We sat looking at Achaia.

It was then that we heard a runner shouting through the camp for the men to meet him, screaming that he had news, that the river had flooded and the plains were mud and the horses were sunk in it up to their bellies, while the chariots were buried up to their axles.

The tide of battle had shifted, the boy said. It now

favored the Israelites, who were comfortable fighting on foot, had been made strong from much running, and were not bothered by the mud.

He said that the Israelites had pressed their advantage, directly confronting the Canaanites for the first time and beating them.

This would not be happy news to many of the wives, who were of Canaanite birth. It was happy news to me, though.

If they won, the Israelites might come to get Achaia. They might have a healer who could help her. They might get her away from Heber and his brutality. They might let me go with them as a slave.

I turned to Latiya. "What do you think of this?"

She said, "I am Kenite. All who have the coin buy from us, so the winners and the losers should matter little enough. I do not think this will affect our trade greatly."

"If Jabin and Sisera lose, and the Israelites take this land, and then Hazor? You don't think that will affect Heber's business?"

"*Heber*'s business, certainly."

I hoped it would. I did not like to think of Latiya or the other wives suffering, or any of the sons. They were, all of them, decent people, hardworking and still kind. I had never been ill-treated by any of them, and as best they could, they had made their stand for me and for Achaia.

They could not control Heber, but they had done

what they could to influence him. It was not their fault it had not been enough.

For a mere concubine, they were doing more than most would, I thought. They were treating her life as if it were something that mattered. I loved them all for that.

The rain fell even harder. We'd pitched our tent on rolling ground that fell away from us at all sides. We had the high ground. Still, I worried that the rain would become so hard, it would flood the floor. Achaia's mat would get soaked, and she would become vulnerable to chills.

Water did seep in at the sides of the tent. I'd hung everything that mattered and that could be damaged by water from the beams across the ceiling. The frame over which we draped the tent was sturdy—pegged wood. It would hold against this torrent.

I heard a groan, and turned.

I discovered that Achaia was turning her head from side to side. Her right hand trailed off the mat and into a little bit of the seeping water.

"Achaia," I called. "Can you hear me?"

She gave me no sign. Still, I could not help but be heartened. She moved and made sounds, and she had done none of that before.

Perhaps . . . . perhaps I dared to hope that she would live to find her freedom after all.

CHAPTER
24

I rose and stepped to the tent flap and stared out at the rain. The miraculous flood filled the air so completely that, should I step out in it for just a moment, I would find myself soaked to the skin before I could step back.

I had never before seen such a rain.

This was my miracle. I was sure of it. The touch of this rain had awakened Achaia. The touch of it might set me free, as well.

Yahweh-Shalom had sent it to bury the chariots and the horses, to give the Israelites a chance to fight in their own element, instead of against men who had better weapons.

If He could send a rain out of season to win a war for His people, if He could wake His daughter Achaia with a touch of rain, this One God could make a miracle for me.

I held out my hand to His rain and let it fall on my palm. Cold. Hard. Cleansing.

I breathed in, and breathed out, and in my heart I asked Yahweh-Shalom to use His power for me— and I again offered myself in the bargain. *Whatever You ask of me, I will do, if You but give me a sign.*

But what sign could He give me? I wondered.

I went back into the tent and sat beside Achaia again. She still lay with her eyes open, her voice a raw croaking noise, her eyes staring at nothing as her head swung from side to side. She didn't know where she was, or what she was doing.

"Talk to me," I told her. "You must hear me. Your ears are not scarred. You must hear that I'm with you. Give me a sign. A little sign. Just squeeze my hand with yours. It's right here. You can do it; I know you can."

She did not squeeze my hand.

I squeezed hers, though, and wished I could reach into her and fix whatever thing Heber had broken.

And then Latiya gasped and hurried to the tent flap. As I turned, she was pulling it shut.

"I must leave you," she said. "As soon as the way is clear, I must return to my own tent and my own husband."

"What's wrong?"

"Fleeing men are running through the camp. If they try to take refuge here—? Well . . . You know what would happen then. They might take us as captives, or use us as they would."

"Your tent will be safer than mine?" I asked her.

"It will be. My husband and my sons are there to protect me."

"I don't know where Heber is," I said. "Why is he not here to protect what is his? Who will stand between these men and Achaia? Who will protect me?"

"Keep your tent flap closed," she told me. "Pray to the gods that you survive this afternoon and night."

I thought of her leaving me to go to safety. And of me, alone in this tent with Achaia, with not even Heber to stand between us and the fleeing Canaanites.

I looked at the row of idols standing in their shrines. I could sacrifice to them and pray for their protection. It would be easy; it would be the thing that the other women in the camp were doing. I could see the Canaanite gods. They were right there in the tent with me, their little painted eyes watching me. I could reach out and touch them.

But they did not live in my heart.

So I prayed again, to Yahweh-Shalom, *her* God who had become mine. "Reach out your hand to us and cover us from the enemy. Give us strength, make us well, keep us safe."

And I felt my heart fill with a courage that was not mine. That had never been mine. I looked down at the blue kuttonet I wore and felt the blossoms of Pigat's headdress brush against my forehead. I was still me, still the thin young woman who had been terrified of her own wedding. I was still afraid.

But a strength coiled inside me, and I knew that if

I reached out my hand, that strength would move it. I knew that I could do things I had never been able to imagine, that I was—at least for that moment— more than I had appeared to be.

I felt like a lioness. I felt certain that Achaia and I would be safe, and that I would be able to stand against any who might come against us, and that I might die doing it, but that if I did, I would give a full accounting for myself.

Feet ran past our tent, very close and very fast, sloshing through the rain-puddled pathways, skittering over the loose stones. I looked around the darkened space. The mallet with which I had hammered in the tent pegs to keep out the rain lay at hand, and the extra tent pegs hung in their bag nearby. I picked up the mallet, hefted it, and felt the comfort of its weight in my hand. Logically, I could look at it and see a good weapon. But I put it back down.

I heard no voice in my head, no words in my heart. But I *knew* that I would not need the mallet to fend off the Canaanites. It was like the feeling of being a lioness that filled me; I was surrounded by fear, and I felt the fear, but somehow I understood that the Canaanite warriors running past the tents, fleeing the pursuing Israelites, were not the trial I would have to face.

Her Yahweh would ask me to make my sacrifice to Him this very day. I knew that, too, though I could no more say how I knew it than I could say how I knew Yahweh was in the tent and watching over Achaia and me.

I closed my eyes and clenched my fists tightly, and I tried to make myself as brave as the spirit of the lioness that filled me. But I could not. I was still afraid.

When I opened my eyes, I was even more afraid. Two Canaanite warriors stood in the women's half of the tent, staring at me. I stared back at them, knowing that they could threaten me, or take me captive, or kill me so that I could not betray the hiding place they had found.

And then they both turned and fled back out of the tent.

He is with me, I thought. *His hand covers me. I do not need to fear.*

I heard no more feet running past our tent.

I returned to Achaia's side and held her hand, and listened to the sounds in the camp. I heard a few screams. Some shouting. The still-steady downpour of the rain.

"We're going to get through this, you and I," I told Achaia. "They'll come for you as they said they would. They'll take you away from here, back to your mother's house, back to your brothers and sisters. You'll be safe some day, and well again. But if you could just wake up, you would be so much easier for them to take away. If you could wake up, I

213

wouldn't be so afraid for you." I squeezed her hand tightly, watching her head roll from side to side. She made whimpering noises, and they were so weak and so heartbreaking, I wanted to cry. How could Heber not feel guilt at what he had done to her. How could he not face punishment for his actions?

Lost in my thoughts, I hesitated for a moment when I felt Achaia's hand squeeze mine.

As I realized what I felt, she spoke.

CHAPTER
25

A chaia's eyes were all the way open, fixed on me. "Help comes," she said.

I stared at her. "I hope so," I told her. "Your people are winning their war, I think. Those fleeing have so far been Canaanites. In all this rain and storm, I don't know if those who would rescue you will find us." And I squeezed her hand. "But . . . you're awake. How do you feel? Can you sit up? Do you hurt?"

She smiled at me, with her split lips and her bruised face, and I wanted so much for Heber to hurt as she hurt. "Help comes," she said again, her voice a hoarse croak. "I must sleep now."

She gave my hand another squeeze, then released it and turned away from me, leaving me alone. I did not want to be alone; I wanted her company, and for her to reassure me that she would be all right, that she would not die of what Heber had done to her.

I would get no such reassurances. Her back was

to me, and her breathing became slow and deep and regular.

But she had spoken. Was that not a miracle? Was that not the hand of her One God holding us up, keeping us safe?

I didn't know. The old women whisper that we get better to die. That before those near death fall from this life into whatever comes after, they brighten, sit up, speak to those to whom they have not spoken in long days or weeks. Their color, the old women say, gets better, and for just a few moments they become themselves again, almost as if they had not been near death.

Hope follows this rally, and their loved ones gather around, breathing easier, believing their sick will be well.

Then they close their eyes to sleep, and never open them again.

The old women say that we get better to die, and I, who had not seen as much death as they, could not refute them. Pigat had done that very thing.

So I watched Achaia sleep, wanting to be comforted, but not daring to let myself be.

The rain had grown lighter, I suddenly realized. It no longer thundered on the tent roof. It no longer roared over the rocky ground of the camp.

I stood and moved cautiously to the tent flap, and dared to peek outside.

The day was not so far gone as I had believed. In places, the clouds had parted; I could see patches of blue sky in between the round, heavy clouds, and as I stood there watching, the blue spread a little and the clouds shrank back.

I caught movement at the corner of my eye and realized that I recognized Sisera; he had been running among the tents. As I watched him, he darted between two of them, looking for a place to hide.

And the lioness courage in my terrified belly and the voice in my heart told me that the time had come for me to move. To act.

I moved.

I ran through the center flap that divided the women's tent from the men's side, and hurried to the flap that opened to the outside. I pulled it back and saw Sisera in the clearing between the entrance to Heber's tent and the entrance to Zimriqart's.

I did not want to say anything. But a vision formed in my mind—of me, of Sisera, of Achaia lying hurt and perhaps dying on the mat on the other side of the tent—and I said, softly, "My lord Sisera, great general and friend and brother of my husband, you look for someone."

He jumped and turned, and in his eyes I could see the fear of hunted things who hear the barking dogs drawing nigh. He stared at me, frowning, and after an instant, said, "I know you."

"I am Jael, wife of Heber, my lord. You seek a place to come in out of the weather? A place of silence and privacy?"

Still staring at me, wary as the cornered calf facing the slaughter, he merely nodded.

"Turn aside, my lord. Turn aside to me. Have no fear. Be welcome in my husband's house," I told him. "You are his friend; he is not within, but he would not wish me to leave you to the rain and to your enemies."

He followed me, stepping within the walls and out of sight, and stood before me, the great general Sisera, the man who had stolen Achaia away from her family, who had killed her father, who bragged of the concubines he took away for himself. He was of my people. He worshipped the same gods I had once worshipped. He was both the friend and the favored and best client of my husband, and I knew that for that alone, I should show him great kindness and do him honor.

Within me, though, lay the spirit of the lioness. Waiting, watching, with sharpened claws, lurking in the tall grass.

Still wild-eyed with fear, Sisera said, "If any come looking for me, hide me."

I nodded. "I will do as you ask, my lord."

And he asked me, "Have you any water? I have been running far, and I thirst."

"I will bring you drink fit for a general," I told

him, ducking my head. "Wait for me—I will be but a moment."

He waited, standing by the closed flap of my husband's tent, peering out from time to time. Nervous. Twitching.

I stepped into the women's side of the tent, and there before me sat the fine blue kos that had been a gift from Levi of Kadesh. I picked it up—it was a beautiful thing, the finest drinking bowl we had. I looked at the water, and then at our skin full of halab, milk with curds. I poured the halab into the bowl for Sisera, and stood for an instant admiring the prettiness of the white on blue.

Then I tucked a tent peg beneath my hagora, the embroidered sash that bound my blue kuttonet at the waist, and in the other side I tucked the mallet, and arranged the folds of hagora and kuttonet to best hide them.

Blue is the color of the covenant between Yahweh-Shalom and his people; it is the place where he touches the sky and the sky touches the water and the water touches us. Blue is the thread that binds us, and I wore blue, and I carried Levi's blue bowl, and I had within me the heart of the lioness, so that even though fear so consumed me that I scarce could breathe, still my hands did not shake as I carried the halab out to Sisera, and offered it to him.

"For you, my lord Sisera," I said, and offered him the bowl.

He looked away from the gap in the tent flap, away from his fears, and after an instant his eyes focused on what I had brought him. He smiled—that cruel, superior smile that I had so often seen on his face—and he nodded. "You know the wife's place," he said. "To honor her husband's guests, to treat them well. This is a good thing. You were well-trained."

He took the bowl from me. Our hands touched as I passed it to him; his were hard and callused, big and strong. He was a big man, Sisera—bigger than Heber, and broader, with muscles hard beneath his fat from swinging a sword. He ate the best foods, drank the best wine—but beneath the fat that marked his wealth, he was still a warrior, with a warrior's eyes. He grinned at me as he took the bowl, and I pulled away, my heart in my throat.

"Your husband does not sufficiently appreciate your many good qualities, I think," he said, and in his compliment, I felt a threat. I ducked my head, making myself seem to be the woman who knew her place, compliant and quiet—and he laughed.

In my heart, the lioness unsheathed her claws. In my heart, the courage that I had never felt before stirred. The hand of Yahweh-Shalom held me up and surrounded me. The One God of the Israelites protected me.

Sisera, father-killing, daughter-stealing Sisera, was the sacrifice I was to make.

Sisera lifted the bowl to his lips, tipped it up to drink of it, and as he did, I put one hand to the mallet and the other to the stake.

And when he closed his eyes for but a moment, I lifted the stake to his head and with the mallet swung thrice.

With the first strike, I drove the stake into his skull, and his eyes flew open.

With the second swing, I forced the stake deeper, and the mighty Sisera's fingers went limp, and the bowl dropped to the floor, spilling milk and curds across my husband's fine rug.

With the third swing, I pounded the stake level, and Sisera's knees collapsed, and he fell to the ground, face forward, slowly, as if he were a great cedar toppled by small men.

With the mallet still in my hand, with the lioness still in my heart, I stared at what I had done, and I was exultant. He was an evil gone from the world. He would never kill another young girl's father, nor would he ever carry that girl screaming from her home, to claim her for his amusement or that of his friends.

The mighty Sisera lay dead at my feet, my duty done for Yahweh-Shalom.

I had done His bidding, I had answered His request. I had not failed.

But if this Israelite God was truly the One God, and if He chose to honor the request of a humble worshipper, a mere woman not even of His own people, yet would He still be hard-pressed to keep me safe beyond that moment?

My husband's dear friend and best customer lay on Heber's floor in Heber's tent, and I, Heber's wife, had killed the man. I could not claim some provocation—there was no provocation sufficient for a woman to kill the king's favored general and live to tell the story. I could hide the mallet, of course, or claim to know nothing of what had happened to Sisera. Could claim that his enemies had caught up with him and slaughtered him—and perhaps I would be believed, though a tent peg and a mallet were no warrior's weapons.

And Sisera lay atop a blue kos from my household that had been the gift of an Israelite, and which was unlike anything anywhere else within the camp. Sisera lay in a puddle of milk and curds. The tent peg in his skull was one of ours.

I could hide Sisera's body under a blanket, then try to get other women in the camp to help me drag him out beyond the edge of the camp, where the jackals and the vultures would feast on him, and no one, perhaps, would even know that he was dead, or where he had gone.

Should Heber be struck mute, I might hope to say that Heber had killed Sisera in a disagreement over money owed, and that would be a little more believable than that the greatest general of the Canaanite army had been felled by some old smith's young wife. But Heber wouldn't be struck mute, and as long as his tongue worked, he would be able to claim that he had never raised a hand against Sisera.

I could say many things that might be believed, some things that probably wouldn't, or I could tell the truth. That I had killed King Jabin's favorite general alone, by myself.

The truth would not set me free. The truth would brand me a murderess and give the husband who hated me a clear path to be freed of me.

I was a woman. For the truth, I would be stoned.

I could run, I thought.

I stood staring down at dead, ugly Sisera, his face no longer red but gray, thinking that if Achaia were awake and well, I could take her and her bag, and the two of us could flee toward the oncoming Israelite army, and beg sanctuary.

But I could not carry Achaia and run. And I would not leave her. I would not abandon my friend and sister to Heber's wrath.

In my heart, the lioness still roared. Her claws were bloodied, her teeth reddened with the blood of the enemy.

I lifted my head. They would have the truth from me, and they could make of it what they would, Heber and his sons. I had done what I had done, and the hand of Yahweh wrapped round me still. I did not think He would honor a liar, but hoped He would protect the truthful.

Outside the tent, at a distance, I heard a man with an accent like Achaia's shouting, asking if anyone had seen the general Sisera.

And I heard a woman's voice responding to his—a stern voice, saying, "He is near."

CHAPTER

26

The two people coming had to be Israelites, didn't they? The fleeing Canaanites were long gone, or if they were not, they had taken refuge in our tents and were hiding, silent and cowering, that they might not be found.

I stood for a moment, holding my breath, unsure what I should do or what I should say.

But then I forced myself to breathe, and I stepped out of Hebes's tent, out of the dark space into the long light of late day, with the sky clearing quickly, with the ground drying. A man and a woman faced me. The man was sturdy, scarred, browned by the sun, his hair black with streaks of gray.

The woman was small, but that was not the first thing I noticed about her. I noticed her eyes. They were light, as if some of the sun reflected in them. She wore a hooded cloak, which kept her face in shadows, but I could not look away from her eyes.

She held a staff in her right hand, but she did not lean on it.

She seemed to me both strong and fierce; if I carried within me the lioness's heart, this woman wore her eyes.

"You have come seeking the fleeing general, the commander of your enemies," I said. I'd meant it as a question, but it did not come out as one.

"Yes," the woman said. The man beside her said nothing, though he glanced down at her, interest marking his face.

"Come, and I will show you the man whom you are seeking."

I turned and walked back into Heber's tent. The two strangers followed me. Perhaps I would have been wise to fear them. After all, I did not know them. They could have been anyone, on this day when friends turned into enemies, and enemies fell around us like rain.

But in the woman's fierce gaze, I saw the new part of myself, the part that had never been there before, but would I thought never leave me again. I knew this woman somehow, and I felt certain that she knew me.

I reached Sisera's body and turned to face them as they entered the tent.

They looked from him to me.

"That is Sisera," the man said.

"It is." The woman threw back the hood of her

cloak. "I saw you," she told me. "From far away, from a time before now, I saw Yahweh ask you to strike Sisera dead. And I saw you obey."

I nodded. She was something other than just a woman, this stranger. She looked at me, and as she did, she looked through me. In all my life, I had never been so certain that someone knew who I was, knew what I'd done, knew *me*, as I was standing there at that moment facing that stranger.

"I am Deborah," she told me. "I am a judge, and a prophetess. A seer. Yahweh the One God speaks to me in visions."

"I know Yahweh," I said, in that moment brave enough to admit that I had turned aside from the idols of my people. "I have prayed daily to him, both for myself and for my sister-by-circumstance, my friend Achaia."

"He has marked you as one of His own," Deborah said. And she turned to the man with her. "This is Barak, the leader of the Israelite warriors, who has this day won a great battle. Whose crowning achievement in that battle, however, goes to you."

Barak's expression as he stood watching me was odd. I saw in his eyes a flash of envy. Calm respect. And, oddly, a hint of sympathy. I did not for a moment think that he, too, knew me. Or that he could see through me the way I felt certain Deborah the judge and prophetess could see through me. But in that instant he and I shared an odd bond.

Other men came through the camp, shouting for
Barak and Deborah, and Barak called them in.
Someone—not me—lifted the walls of the tent and
tied them up, putting the tent pegs away as if he had
spent his own life living in such tents. Someone else
stood at the outside of the tent and began waving
people our way. The space filled with Israelites.

Then among their number, I saw Levi of Kadesh.
He was watching me, and I could not turn my eyes
away from him. He was so beautiful, for all that he
was filthy and rain-sodden and bloodied. He smiled
at me, and I smiled back, and began to cry, silently,
both at the same moment.

Deborah cleared a space, and Barak moved beside
her—and they began to sing a battle song, while the
men with me gathered up the body of Sisera, dead
by my hand, and while Levi knelt on the ground,
where Sisera's blood had mixed with the milk that
had spilled, and lifted up the bowl that he had given
me. He stared into my eyes, holding that bowl, and
the war song of Deborah and Barak faded in my ears.

In a perfect world, I would have been born to
Levi's people. In a perfect world, my parents would
have given me in marriage to him. In a perfect world,
we would share a future of love and laughter and
fat babies—but we did not live in a perfect world.

We did not live in a perfect world, but in the world
where Sisera's blood soaked into the carpet that belonged to my husband, Heber, who hated me and

who would finally have justification for seeing me dead. We lived in the world where I had killed a general, and that might have made me a hero to Deborah and Barak, but it would not make me a hero to Heber, who had counted on Sisera's trade to fill his tent with luxury, and on Sisera's influence to reflect on him and make Heber an important man, too.

In the world we lived in, Levi would go his way, and I would stay behind with Heber, and I would face the death that I had earned.

I could—faintly, and as if from far, far away—hear Kenite men with Kenite accents shouting for Heber even as I stood there. As I yearned for a man and a life I could not have.

As strangers filled my husband's tent.

In my ear, a man whispered, "Quick, where is Achaia, the daughter of Leoboam, stolen from her home by Sisera."

"She lies on the other side of the tent, hurt by Heber the night past. I have not had time to check on her the past little while; she had started seeming healthier, but I am shamed to say I do not know how she is now. The bag by her head, though, holds her belongings. Take it when you take her."

He vanished. I never saw his face. I could not look away from Levi, who stood beside the blood, beside the milk, holding the blue bowl. I could not turn my eyes away.

I heard Deborah's clear voice sing:

Most blessed of women be Jael,
the wife of Heber the Kenite,
of tent-dwelling women most blessed.
He asked water and she gave him milk,
She brought him curds in a lordly bowl.
She put her hand to the tent peg, and her right hand
*   to the workmen's mallet;*
She struck Sisera a blow,
She crushed his head,
She shattered and pierced his temple.
He sank, he fell,
He lay still at her feet;
At her feet he sank, he fell;
And where he sank, there he fell dead.

Levi's eyebrow arched in query; had this been me, this woman that Deborah sang of, this fierce killer of a murderous general? Did she sing true?

I nodded. I did not ask myself how Deborah knew what I had done, how she had seen it as clearly as if she had been there. She was Yahweh's prophetess. Her lioness eyes saw far beyond the moment and the place.

I only looked at Levi, who, when I nodded, smiled at me with warmth and pride.

Why? Why could I not have been his?

I did not have long to consider that. A moment, perhaps.

Then Heber returned, loud and furious and clearly

full of wine. He pushed his way through the strangers, shouting at them to get out of his tent, shouting that no man should have to return to his home to find it filled with men he did not know, and in the midst of this, he came face-to-face with dead Sisera, who was lying on the small cart. The Israelite warriors were getting ready to remove the body—though I could not begin to guess what they would do with it. Sisera would have taken the head of his enemy, had he been alive and Barak dead, and would have paraded it around the camp on a pike, and then through the streets of Hazor, and would at last have stuck it at the front gate of Hazor for all to see, that they could know the might of Sisera, and be afraid.

Perhaps these warriors planned something similar.

But their plans were not a matter to interest Heber. The death of Sisera was, though.

He stopped, seeing the still-open eyes of the man he knew, seeing the blood at Sisera's mouth and the grayness of his skin.

"What happened here?" he shouted, and for a long moment, when no one spoke, I could only hope that no one would. I wanted Heber never to know what had happened.

But of course, the fact that I had killed Sisera was not a thing that would stay secret. How could it? What I had done had changed the course of the war. The Israelites had no one except for King Jabin himself left to stand against them—they would not keep silent about the woman who had removed their enemy of twenty years.

Heber's gaze fell on me, and the lioness courage within me faltered. All around me, a silence fell.

"You let these people in?" he asked me.

"I did, my lord husband," I admitted. "I asked Sisera to take shelter in your tent, as well."

He returned his gaze to the dead body, and then shook his head as if to clear it of the haze of wine. "He was my friend and brother," Heber told me after a pause. "You did right to offer him shelter. But if you then let in the ones who killed him . . ."

"I did not do that," I said.

"Good."

And within me, the lioness roared once more, not done with me, not satisfied with the blood already on her claws. "I killed him myself," I said.

CHAPTER

27

I almost thought my words had struck a kindred blow to the mallet I had swung against Sisera, so hard did this news strike Heber. His head jerked; his face turned a dark and meaty red; his knees sagged so that he had to grab hold of the cart in which Sisera lay to steady himself.

"Tell me, woman, what you just said."

"I killed Sisera," I repeated. "I gave him milk to drink, and while he drank it, I took a tent peg and with a mallet drove it into his skull."

Heber began to tremble. "Why!" he screamed at me. "Why would you do such a thing, you stupid woman?" His face grew even redder; his hands clenched the cart; his knuckles turned white. I had seen him furious many times. But never had I seen him like this. I would not be stoned by all the men of the camp, I realized. Heber was going to rush me and kill me where I stood.

"It was the will of Yahweh-Shalom, the One True

God, that he die," I said. "For all his evils, for all his wrongs, Sisera was judged and found guilty. Mine was not the hand that judged him, but mine was the hand that slew him."

I could see white all the way around the irises in Heber's eyes. I could see spittle bubbling at the corners of his mouth. "You serve Baal," he screamed at me. "You serve Baal and El and Mot, Asherah, Anat, and Ashtartu. You are my wife, you worship my gods, you are not some Israelite whore who offers your prayers to some worthless, idol-less god!"

"I pray to Yahweh," I said. "Achaia taught me the truth of the One God."

His eyes went dark and ugly, and Heber stormed past the men in the tent, past Deborah the judge and prophetess, past Levi, who watched him with one hand on the hilt of his sword, past me. Heber stormed into the women's side of the tent and began to scream, "Where is she? Where is my faithless, barren, Israelite concubine?"

"She was taken as the spoils of war," Barak said. His voice carried into the other side of the tent—no one else was making a sound.

Heber exploded back into the men's side of the tent, scattering pillows and lamps and the gifts and decorations that important men accumulate. He came into the room like a storm and shouted at Barak, "Who are you to tell me that what I own has been taken from me? Who?"

"I am Barak, son of Abinoam," Barak said, and his voice was, if anything, softer, calmer, and yet somehow more deadly. "I am the general who led the Israelites against the Canaanites; I am the general who this day all but won the war . . . though the final victory goes to your wife, Jael, may her name be praised."

And that name—*Barak*—spoke to Heber. He said, "Ah." And after a moment, "Oh." And then, a moment later, "Well."

Heber was a foul man, but he was also cunning. He could smell which way the breeze blew, he could read the sign of a shift in the river's flow.

And Sisera lay dead, and in Heber's tent stood the man whose army had conquered Sisera's.

And armies needed weapons, didn't they? And weapons needed smiths to forge them.

Heber studied me, and in his dark, beady eyes, I could see calculation. I had killed the general Sisera; but Sisera had already lost the war. So, in a way, I had removed a liability. I had moved Heber from the side of the losers to the side of the winners. I claimed to worship the God of the Israelites. I could be an asset. I could be worth a steady flow of trade if he could just find the right angle with these customers.

And his eye lit on Levi, who held the bowl he had given as a gift. Levi, who had received from Heber a sword worth much more that what he had paid.

235

Levi would surely tell Barak that Heber was a good man, and honorable. Worth doing business with.

All that I could see in my husband's face.

Heber turned to me, and any anger he felt on the inside he had hidden. No matter how drunk he was, he was a trader first, able to calculate the advantage in a situation in an instant.

He said, "Then, my beloved wife, you have done good this day. You have brought honor on our house—you have won a great victory." He didn't quite choke on those words, but almost.

"You would so quickly deny your dearest friend, your brother, your greatest customer, the mighty Sisera?" I asked. I cannot say what prompted me to goad him, except perhaps the sharp claws of my lioness.

He looked startled. "I did much business with Sisera," he said, waving his hands as if to hurry that inconvenient fact on its way. "I did much business with any who would pay me."

"But better business for Sisera than for the rest," Levi said, watching Heber, watching me.

Heber turned to Levi with a hurt expression on his face. "You wound me through the heart," he said. "The fine sword you carry, forged of the iron of kings, was worth ten times what you paid me for it. You paid for a bronze sword. Have you forgotten the way you were treated?" he asked. "How I feasted you and made you a guest in my home, how I called you friend. You could suggest about me such unkind things, after all I did for you?"

"Shall I tell him what you said behind his back, my husband? Shall I tell this warrior how you laughed at making him come once each month to the Kenite camp, promising each time that the sword for which he had already paid you would be done. How each month, he came and the sword was not done, not because you had not time to make it, but only because he was one of the Israelites, and you thought it funny to toy with him in front of Sisera and King Jabin and your other Canaanite customers."

"Wife," Heber said, "you have had a difficult day. Go now to your side of the tent, and be silent. You have been overtired."

Barak said, "I would hear what she has to say."

Heber looked torn. Clearly he did not want to offend this important man, who could become a major client replacing the dead Sisera and the defeated King Jabin. But he didn't want anyone to hear anything else that might come out of my mouth, either, since I was so clearly not being the obedient wife I was supposed to be. He picked his way carefully through the lion traps; he said, "She speaks nonsense. I will deal with her later. I have had only respect for all my customers, and will not have a woman's lying tongue suggest otherwise."

From the back of the tent, I heard the voice of Latiya, the wife of Zimriqart. "But all that Jael says is true. All of us heard the story of how, when you found that the warrior Levi of Kadesh was in fact looking in secret into supplying weapons for all of Barak's army, you suddenly made him a sword far greater than the worth of his trade. But you did it only because you hoped to win the trade of Barak. All of us heard you laughing at the humiliation you caused him before you found the truth about him. Every one of your sons heard you laughing about him making the trip each month and getting nothing in return. Every one of your grandsons, as well. And most of the smiths back in the Kenite camp, should anyone care to ask them." She paused, while I watched Heber's face begin turning that ugly red again. And then she said, "But every woman in this camp heard what you said, as well. We hear your words, we speak your language, we are not deaf, for all that we say little."

"You say too much," he said, staring through the crowd that had parted to make room for her. He glared at her with hatred in his eyes, and when he stared at me, the look was twice as deadly.

He would kill me that night; I could see it. When the Israelites had taken their spoils of war and picked clean the bodies of their enemies and hunted down the last of the Canaanite warriors who had sought hiding places within our camp, they would leave.

And then Heber would beat me to death. He

would finish with me what he had started with Achaia.

I thought of Achaia, who might get better, but who might still die. If she died without waking again, her people would never know why. And they needed to know what had happened to her. They deserved to know.

I lifted my chin and gave Heber a cold smile. He could only kill me once. Then I turned my face to Barak and said, "Ask him how Achaia, his Israelite concubine, came to be in this tent. Ask him how she came to be so badly hurt."

There was a quick conference among the strangers gathered in the tent, most of it seeming to center on Deborah. "She was the young woman claimed as spoils of war, who will be taken home to her family, is she not?" Deborah asked the warriors around her.

She received a number of quick affirmatives.

The prophetess Deborah lifted her staff, and the talk within the tent died. Every eye watched her; every ear listened to her words.

"You have claimed to be a friend of our people, an ally. You claim that you have done well by our people, that you have given better than asked of you, that you have called some of our number friend and brother. So I would have your story, Heber, son of Hebaal. How came this woman to be in your possession, and how came she to be so ill-used and so grievously wounded when we claimed her?"

Heber looked at the prophetess with ill-disguised disdain. He did not speak to her, but to Barak. "Your woman," he said, "overreaches her authority. Perhaps you should send her to the women's side of the tent with my wife, and instruct her to cook you a meal after your long day of fighting."

Several of the Israelites put hand to sword at those words; others coughed suspiciously and turned their faces away. Heber did not seem to understand who it was that faced him, or what her staff meant, or in what regard the men around her held her.

"The woman," Barak said in a voice kept low and even, but edged with sharpened iron, "is the prophetess and judge, Deborah, who sits in judgment over Israel. The men and the women of Israel come to her feet to hear her words and be judged."

"Men who listen to the words of a woman are fools," Heber said.

Swords came halfway out of sheaths at that point, but Barak raised a hand, and his warriors calmed themselves. "If we are fools," Barak said, "still we are the fools who this day won this land in battle with her guidance, and who now rule over those who dwell within it. Our judge has become your judge, Heber, son of Hebaal, and she has asked of you two questions: How did our daughter Achaia come to live under your roof as your concubine, and how did she obtain the grievous wounds that she bore when we reclaimed her this very day?"

Fear had found its way at last into Heber's wine-addled mind—fear and realization that the men who had supported him were dead or taken captive, and that the men he had misused had taken the places his allies had once held.

So he told just as much of the truth as he had to, and twisted that with as many lies as he dared.

CHAPTER
28

Heber said, "Sisera stole the maiden Achaia away from her home—she was part of the spoils of war," he said. "And . . . he paid me part of his debt with her. He owed a great deal, Sisera did, and I did not want the girl. I told him I wanted metal—silver and iron—but he said he had not enough to pay all that he owed unless he also gave me the girl." Heber shrugged, trying to look nonchalant. "I took her. And was kind to her.

"I treated her as well as a husband treats a favorite wife—she had good food and good clothing, jewelry to wear, trinkets and bangles and combs for her hair.

"But when our camp was attacked by bandits," he continued, warming to his tale, "they came into my tent. They used and misused her. I did not turn away from her then, though other men had despoiled her, but kept her in my tent, and my wife tended her, and we hoped that she would one day be well again."

I was stunned by the breadth of his lies. Did he

think I would agree with him? Yes, of course he did, for he intended to kill me if I did not.

And he intended to kill me anyway. I, who could only die once.

I opened my mouth to argue with him—to tell the truth. But Deborah raised her staff, and again all within the tent fell silent. I held my tongue, waiting to see what she would say.

"I have listened to the testimony of Heber, son of Hebaal, and I have seen the girl Achaia, and I have heard the voice within my soul—the word of the Lord has writ itself upon my heart. Hear me, then."

The Israelites and Kenites in the tent, and those crowded outside it, seemed to me to hold their breath.

Deborah pointed at Heber. "You received our daughter Achaia as a gift from the general Sisera, not as payment. She was, further, a gift you welcomed— but one you misused. And no harm came to her on the day bandits attacked this camp; the injuries she bore were fresh, given no earlier than last night. Her bruises have not aged or yellowed, nor have her cuts begun to heal. She bore on her face the marks of a man's fist—these are marks I have seen before, and I know the look of them well enough."

Deborah planted the staff on the ground before her with a finality that spoke of both confidence and anger, and wrapped both her hands around it, and leaned forward. "The young woman Achaia has suf-

fered hurt from no one but you, Heber, son of Hebaal, and only you will pay the penalties for your
actions. So do I judge this."

Heber stared at her, his mouth gaping. Then he
turned to me, his face twisted with fury, and snarled,
"You *told* her. You told this witch what I did; you
betrayed me; you have betrayed your husband to
strangers, woman, and I will see that you pay for
your betrayal with your life. There are laws that deal
with women like you."

I grinned at him, though I must have looked like
a madwoman doing it. "From the dust, Heber, my
bones will laugh at you. My charred skull will watch
you in your poverty, and it will mock you until the
day you die. You have no great general anymore to
make you rich, nor have you the favor of a king to
protect you from your actions. You have no concubines to pamper you, no wives save me to cook or
spin or sew for you, no sons who will stand by you,
no daughters to tend you in your declining years.
Everyone who once cared for you, you have turned
against you. You will die poor, and alone, and with
my laughter ringing in your ears."

"But you will die first," he said.

"She will not," Deborah said. "At least not by your
hand. You have no grounds upon which to claim the
right of her death." She paused a moment, looking at
me thoughtfully. "You have a solid case to divorce her,
though. I think all of us here today have seen that."

Heber stared from Deborah to me, then back to Deborah.

"Divorce her. Divorce her?" He stood for a moment, considering that. "I could divorce her. And then she would be husbandless, and shamed. She's barren—no man would take her. She is a betrayer of her husband, a betrayer of her gods, a murderess, a treacherous monster. I could divorce her and send her out into the wilderness to be devoured by jackals. I can let Mot decide her fate. I can let Baal, from whom she turned her face, decree her death."

I thought I saw the faintest curl of a smile flicker at the corners of Deborah's lips. Then it was gone, and she said, "You could do that."

"I divorce you, Jael of Hazor," he said, staring at me. "I divorce you." He spat the words out, his voice contemptuous, his lips twisted in a sneer. "I divorce you."

I was, in that moment, divorced, and had not even had the time to consider what that would mean. Everything Heber had said about me was true enough. I'd had my reasons for acting as I had—but I was, in fact, a betrayer of my husband before strangers, a betrayer of the gods of my birth, a murderess, and—if someone wanted to consider the method by which I had gained Sisera's trust before killing him treachery—a treacherous monster.

How strange it is that we rarely see ourselves the way others see us. We put what we have done in a good light for ourselves, never thinking that it will not look the same to others.

How Heber had described me—that was how everyone I had ever known would see me. How my family would see me. My mother, my father, my sisters and brothers. They would not see me as someone brave, or as someone who had done a good thing.

My knees felt weak; I thought I might fall down, and so leaned back, thinking that one of the tent beams was behind me and that I could rest against it. But it wasn't, and I started to fall backward.

Hands caught me. Strong hands. And in my ear, a kind voice that I knew—and had no business yearning after—said, "Steady there. You've done well so far. Be strong a little longer."

Levi set me back on my feet.

Heber looked pleased at my evident distress.

But the business was not yet finished, for Deborah said, "Our people require a written decree of divorce."

"I don't write," Heber said. "Nor do I have a priest in this camp who can write for me."

Fully half the Israelite men around me said, almost at the same instant, "I can write."

One of them stepped forward, while another went off to locate something upon which to write, and writing supplies. I stepped back, one careful step at a time, and leaned myself against the tent pole I thought had been behind me before. And I watched the strangers around me. They seemed quietly pleased. They seemed, in fact, eager to help Heber rid himself of the wife who had shamed and betrayed him.

I did not understand their eagerness. Did they think my parents would welcome me back into their home? Did they think that I would have a place to stay, people who would still care for me after what I had done—after what I had become?

Could they know so little of my people? Or did they not care what became of me?

That seemed possible. I was a stranger to them, and though I had done something they had considered valuable by ridding the world of Sisera, still, I was no one of importance to them. I could not be a hero; I was a woman, a Canaanite, not of their people. No one would remember me after that day. People would remember that Barak had led the war against Sisera and had defeated him. Songs would be written and sung about that.

But that Sisera fell by a woman's hand in a tent at Oak in Zaanannim? No. That would be forgotten in a day. It is the lot of women to be forgotten.

The men who had gone off in search of writing supplies returned. They had with them an ostraca of fired clay, and a reed with the tip cut into a brush, and red ink. And one of them carefully painted characters on the ostraca, painting them slowly, one after the other, and blowing on the ink when he was done to speed its drying.

Then he held it aloft, and read it aloud. "It says, 'I, Heber, son of Hebaal, divorce and put aside my wife, Jael of Hazor.' Can you sign your name?" He offered the reed-brush to Heber.

"I don't write," Heber repeated, looking mulish as he said it.

"Then make a mark upon the ostraca, and I will write that you made the mark, and three other men who are here to watch you make it will write their names in witness. And when that is done, you will be divorced from her."

Heber took the brush then, and at the direction of the makeshift warrior-scribe, carefully painted a straight line, and when he had done that, crossed it at right angles with a second.

Other men gathered round him then, and for a moment there were mutterings as they passed ink and brush, each to the next, and complained about how little space there was to put their names.

And then it was done.

The one who had painted the original decree took it to Deborah and handed it to her. She studied it for a long moment—I wondered if she could read the words written there. I suspected she could. Her eyes held no bewilderment as they looked over the lines of writing, and no uncertainty. She looked up at me, and addressed me directly. "Jael of Hazor, you are divorced." She held out the ostraca to me and said, "Take this and keep it. It is proof, should you ever wish to remarry, that you are free and able by law to do so, and that you have not fled from your husband. And it prevents Heber from changing his mind and claiming that you are not divorced." She smiled a little as she said that. "I suspect you would quickly have reason to wish for it, did you not have it."

I took the square of fired clay and stared down at it. The red lines and swirls meant nothing to me. I knew not which way was the top of them, or which the bottom. But I understood well enough that those lines and swirls meant a form of freedom for me, even if a dangerous one.

Heber could not call me back. He had no say over me any longer. He could not claim that I had wronged him—he had, by divorcing me, given up his right to claim anything about me at all.

I had no place to go, and no one to go to—but I didn't have to stay with Heber anymore.

Couldn't stay with Heber anymore, in fact.

I no longer had a home.

CHAPTER
29

With the ostraca in my hand, I turned to Deborah. "Do I take my belongings? Where do I go? What do I do now?"

If there had been a lioness within me, she had gone into hiding. I could only think that the world was large, and hard, and I was insignificant.

Heber began to laugh. "You got what you deserved. Get out of my tent." He stared belligerently at the men crowding into his tent, and at Deborah, and at the women on the outskirts of the crowd—his daughters-in-law, his granddaughters. "All of you get out. You have no business here."

Deborah said, "Those things that belong to you—your clothing, your jewelry, your combs and weaving goods—are all things that you can take. Those items that are part of your husband's household—cook pots, foodstuffs, and tools—you may not take."

I nodded. If I had a bag, I could pack it as I had the one I had put together for Achaia, only this time it would hold my worldly goods, such as they were. My other kuttonet (the red one I had worn on my wedding day), some jewelry—though none that had first belonged to Pigat—sandals, combs and brush, little pots of kohl and malachite. My spindle and distaff and loom, the piece of cloth I was weaving, perhaps the lovely wool I'd bought but had not yet spun.

It would not fill a large bag; it would require one of a size that a lone woman could easily carry from one end of the earth to the other.

I walked warily past Heber and into the women's side of the tent. It would be empty when I was gone. Not long ago, it had held Pigat and Talliya, Achaia and me, the littlest boys. How quickly things had changed, how quickly they had gone from bright to dark within those walls.

I looked around me, and picked up the small basket where I kept my belongings. The basket would be inconvenient, but it was, for the time being, better than nothing at all. I began putting my wools and weaving tools in it, and heard Heber's voice. "The basket is a household item. It is mine, and you may not take it."

I began pulling my things out of the basket, then, and placing them in a neat pile on my unrolled mattress. The room had grown dark as the sun went down; I lit an oil lamp, and by its flickering light took inventory of the things I could call my own.

They were not much, but they were more than I could carry without basket or bag.

Outside my side of the tent, I heard a cart rattle, and oxen stamp their feet and snort. One of the older granddaughters peeked through the tent flap and said, "There is a cart here to carry away your things, and an empty trunk in which you can put them. I've been asked to tell you to bring them out quickly."

A cart?

Mute, I nodded, and picked up everything I owned in one awkward bundle in my arms. I carried it out, and found an old highland cart waiting, and on it a battered trunk with the lid already opened.

And beside it, Deborah, and Barak, and Levi.

As I put my belongings in, making sure that my divorce decree was there, Deborah said, "You'll stay with me for a little while. I'll send runners to your family, to let them know that you are safe, and what has befallen you. No doubt some sources will make sure what they hear of you is ill; I'll be certain that they hear the truth, and know you for the hero you are."

I didn't know what to say. "I . . . you need not . . . you are . . ."

"You are a hero. An honorable woman. My household will have a place for you so long as you need it." She smiled. "I suspect you may not need it for very long." She glanced at Levi, and Levi smiled at her, and then gave a shy smile to me.

We spent the night in small tents outside Heber's

camp. In the morning, while we packed and readied for the walk to the highlands, Heber's sons packed their camp. I saw Heber packing, too—but where others in the camp worked together, offering each other assistance, and so making short work of the difficult task, no one offered him help. When I walked away, he was struggling by himself to take down and pack away the grand tent that Talliya and Achaia and I had put up with the help of other women in the camp. I did not envy him the task. But I remembered how he had treated Talliya, and how he had treated Achaia, and finally, how he had treated me.

And I did not pity him.

I walked away from the women who had been a part of my life with tears and good wishes. Talliya and I hugged, and she thanked me for standing with her, and begged me to send word of my life, and news of Achaia. Heber's daughters-in-law embraced me, too, and whispered cautious congratulations that I was free of him, and wary hopes that someone might yet care enough for me to offer me marriage and a home . . . and perhaps someday children of my own.

With tears we parted; most of those women who had been my friends I would never see again, no matter where I went. I might hear word of one or another of them, but they would never again be my family. They would be lost to me.

I found myself walking beside Deborah for a while as we headed into the wilderness. Never had I been so certain of my safety; I was surrounded on all sides by men with swords and shields, all of them watching the land around us for any signs of danger.

Deborah said, "You're afraid."

"I don't know what will happen to me now. I had been sure I was going to die—and I was afraid of that. But still, I could see the end of my life and know that all the horrible things would stop happening once I was dead. And it wouldn't be long, I thought."

"And now a whole world of possible horrible things has opened itself up, waiting to devour you."

I nodded.

"I understand that. My own life had its moments of terror. Perhaps I shall tell you the story some day." She smiled at me, and said, "I will hear you if you call to me, but I must walk for a while with Barak— we have much to discuss concerning the future of this land. Walk a while without me, and know that in the near future, at least, you have a place to stay and food to eat and friends who will care for you." She patted me on the shoulder, then hurried ahead.

I followed the cart that held my belongings.

And suddenly I was no longer alone.

Levi of Kadesh walked beside me.

My heart began to skip and race, and my breath came fast.

"Have you any dreams, Jael?" he asked me.

I looked over at him, but felt the heat rising to my cheeks, and looked quickly down at my feet. "When I sleep at night," I said.

"That isn't what I mean. Have you any hopes for your future? When you imagined your life, how did you think it would be?"

Ah. Those sorts of dreams. I'd buried them when I discovered what Heber was, and when I knew that I would never be free of him.

Now I was free of him. But I was a divorced woman—shamed, ruined, my reputation in tatters. Dreams such as those I had once so innocently held were as far beyond my reach as the sun that hung in the sky.

I did not intend to tell him. But to my horror, I heard my voice say, "I thought I would have a house full of children. That I would have a husband who shared his life and his laughter with me, as well as his hopes and his fears. I thought that I would cook and clean, and spin and sew, that I would dye wool as my mother does, and as her mother did before her, and that I would make a good home for the people I loved. I wanted the sort of life my parents have."

He walked beside me for a while, quiet. I could feel him watching me, but I did not look up. I felt foolish for telling him the truth.

"You were brave, Jael, to face a hardened warrior

and kill him. You were brave to face your husband, believing that he would kill you, and tell the truth about what he did." He laughed. "And you were clever and kind to spread that rumor about me being someone of importance, so that I finally received a sword. I never forgot your kindness, or the quickness of your wit."

Still I did not look up at him. "I . . . acted as my heart bade me act."

"You have a good heart. Mothers should be courageous, to protect their children. Wives should be kind, to make the home a good place. You've changed. No longer are you the timid, fragile dove. You remind me of . . . a lioness."

Inside me, something shivered awake—a sense that he had seen through me the day before, that he knew me better than he possibly could.

He said, "Lionesses who are fierce and devoted to their cubs see their offspring survive. The cubs of those lionesses who are weak or cowardly or distracted die, prey to a thousand enemies." He paused, and I heard him draw a slow, deep breath. I glanced over at him and saw that he no longer looked in my direction. He stared off at the approaching hills, his brow furrowed. "My people have a thousand enemies, Jael. If we are to survive, our men must be lions and our women lionesses."

And then he looked over and his gaze caught mine and held it.

"I would have you as my wife, if you would have me as your husband. I would be kind. I would, Yahweh willing, give us both a house full of children. I would treat you as the other half of me, not as my servant." He laughed nervously, and looked down at the ground. "I cannot tell you the guilty nights I spent dreaming of you, and praying that I could either forget you or find someone so like you that I could be honorable before the Lord and men, and yet my heart could be happy. I did not dare to pray that you might be set free—no good man can pray for his own joy at the expense of another's misery. But Yahweh sometimes gives us more than we ask, in ways that we could not imagine."

I looked up at him, and dared speech again. "I dreamed of you, as well, though I put you aside in my dreams. I made promises, and I intended to keep them."

"Could you dare to make them again?"

I walked beside him, staring at the rough hills, thinking about the future, and about the past—about my parents and the rest of my family, about what they would think of me. I wondered if they could wish me well. I wondered if I might hope to dare for joy in my life; if I might look at the future and think of it filled with more than barest, grittiest survival.

I thought of Achaia, too—on her way to her family by a different route than our party took. If I could find hope, could she? Might she yet be well, and loved, and cared for? Might she regain the life Sisera and then Heber took from her?

"Would you marry me?" Levi asked again.

CHAPTER
30

Almost two years have passed since my long walk through the wilderness as a newly divorced woman with a second wilderness in my heart.

I sit with my son Abisha in my arms—his name means "Yahweh's gift," and I believe with all my heart that his father Levi should have been given the same name. Abisha is beautiful, with his father's dark eyes and curling hair and wide, bright smile.

The sunlight falls through my window onto my spinning—blue thread of linen, fine and strong, that glows like sapphires in the light of late day. I have already made our bread, and the rich scents of our late meal as it cooks fill the walls of our house. Outside, in the street, young boys and girls laugh and shout as one of their number kicks a leather ball from foot to foot, never letting it touch the ground. I can see him. Some day, perhaps, my son will do the same thing.

My parents came to the village to see me wed, as

did Deborah, with whom I lived while we made all the preparations. I have had word that my mother and sister will be returning after the next harvest. My father met a young man from the village who offered for my sister, and my parents, after getting to know him, and after seeing the way we live here, agreed to accept his offer.

She will live near me; our children will get to grow up together.

Up the street, Achaia walks, wearing green, her hair tied back and the bracelets at her wrists and ankles jangling. She sees me watching out the window and breaks into a run, her smile flashing.

Achaia will wed before the harvest; her husband-to-be is young, and the two of them will have little to begin with, but her husband has great skill with wood—he carves and builds the finest furniture I have ever seen. They may be poor to start with, but I think they will do well.

She leans in the window, and first looks at Abisha. "He's so fat," she says, laughing at his greedy nursing. "He'll be tall as Levi before you can blink." And then she gives me a conspiratorial smile. "Levi was at the market, and he's on his way home now, bringing a present for you. I promised I would not tell you what it was . . . but it is *so* beautiful."

And then she glances down the street. "I have to run. He'll be coming any moment, and I don't want him to think I've spoiled his surprise." And she darts away, toward the home of her future sister-in-law, where Achaia and her mother and her rescued sisters have been staying while they prepare for the wedding feast. Her brothers have talked of moving to this village, too, so that their widowed mother could be close to her daughters as well as her sons.

I watch Achaia leave, and rock my son in my arms, and await the light of my day, whose smile is the first thing I see each morning, and the last thing I see each night: My Levi is as much a gift as my son.

Yahweh is good, and each day and each night, I give thanks—not just for the joy I have now, but also for the pain and the suffering that brought me to this place that is so full of hope and life. I could never have had this joy without the sorrow that came first; I could never have appreciated what a gift Levi was had I not first suffered through what a bad husband could be.

No gift should be taken for granted, but received and appreciated with deep and heartfelt thanks.

Afterword

Jael's story in the Bible is both short and contradictory. In Judges 4:21, she waits until Sisera is asleep before driving the tent peg into his head. But in the Song of Deborah (Judges 5)—which is a much older text than the later prose description of events—Deborah clearly states that Sisera was quite awake when Jael killed him—that "he sank, he fell, he lay at her feet . . ." after she hammered the tent peg into his head. Judges 5:27)

I chose to write the story based on the older text because it was closer to the source of the events as they happened. I also find Jael's actions much more courageous when taken against a warrior wide awake than against a sleeping victim.

Beyond the bare skeleton of Jael's actions, however, we know little. We know that the Israelites and the Kenites did not get along particularly well, that at the same time that the Kenites (a tribe of smiths) were dealing with the Israelites, they were also dealing with the Canaanites. We know that Jabin had been at war against Barak for about twenty years.

But we don't know who Heber was, or who his father was. There are respectable sources, in fact, that suggest that, since the translation of *heber* is "a group," the phrase that has been translated "Jael, wife of Heber of the Kenites," in fact should read, "Jael, woman of the group of Kenites."

The odds are good that she was pagan—the Kenites were more closely allied to the Canaanites than to the Israelites, and in this time period, the Israelites were having problems among their own people with Baal worship. So I used this opportunity to dig out and present some of the scholarship on Canaanite worship, because it was something Israelites dealt with and because it makes a good contrast for the religion of Yahweh.

To say that I have taken liberties with Jael's story is to understate the case hugely. I have, though, done my best to illustrate the world of women living in a tent village in an era when polygamy was acceptable among the rich and women were the fair spoils of war, and to demonstrate how an insignificant member of a tribe not a part of Israel could become a heroine remembered thousands of years after her death.

Ann Burton
May 28, 2005

Discussion Guide

1. Jael's parents chose her husband for her, which was customary at the time. She had no say in the matter, and though her parents did as well as they could for her, she had no recourse when it became clear that their choice had been a poor one. Imagine yourself in a world where your first meeting with your husband or wife could be on your wedding day. Consider what your life might be like, and how you would deal with problems if you had no power to get free of them.

2. While polygamy was not common among the poor in Jael's day, it was acceptable for men who were rich enough to support more than one wife, plus the resulting children. The family dynamics of sharing one husband among two or more wives or concubines would be challenging. Place yourself in Jael's situation, imagining that you are the new wife. Or consider being the husband

supporting multiple wives and concubines, or the child with so many adults to answer to and so many siblings of various degrees always around. How would you deal with jealousy, lack of privacy, and the other issues that would face you?

3. In Jael's world, in most places and most cases, adultery carried a death penalty. In theory, women and men were held equally responsible for adultery. In fact, however, men were rarely punished, while women almost always were. Even today, in some cultures and some parts of the world, women receive the death penalty for adultery, for premarital sex, and even for having been raped. What cultures require this, and why?

4. Israelite law (Deuteronomy 21:10–14) gave a woman taken as spoils of war certain rights: She could belong only to her captor or one of his sons; she had to be given a month of mourning for her lost family before she would be required to act as a concubine or wife; she could not be sold if she did not please her captor, but had to be freed. By the standards of the time, these were enlightened laws. Consider how they differ from the treatment women in war-ravaged countries receive today.

5. Women in Jael's era were responsible not just for preparing meals, but also for maintaining food

supplies, in places lacking grocery stores, where some food had to be tended on the hoof and slaughtered at the time of use—or milked—and other food had to be grown in the backyard or bought from irregular supplies. How would you manage to keep yourself and a family fed under these conditions, and how does it differ from how you and your family eat today?

6. Dyeing, spinning, and weaving were skills that women made use of regularly to keep themselves and their families clothed—but they were also a source of comfort and pride. In what skills do you find comfort and pride? What would you like to learn to do that would benefit not just yourself but those around you, as well?

7. Heber and his sons were skilled tradesmen, with talent sought out by men of different beliefs and creeds. They were willing to sell to both sides in the ongoing war; how are they alike (and how are they different from) arms dealers and governments today who do the same things?

8. Achaia maintained her beliefs even in a situation where she risked her life to do so. Have you ever been faced with a situation where your life was endangered by what you believed? How did you (or would you) deal with such a situation?

9. Jael was faced with several emergency situations

in which she had to act quickly and correctly to save a life. What skills do you have with which you could do the same thing, if no one else was around to help you? Do you know, or have you considered learning, such skills as the Heimlich maneuver, rescue breathing, and CPR?

10. When Jael killed Sisera, she made herself a criminal in the eyes of some and a hero in the eyes of others. Sisera's actions and position made him an enemy of Israel; and from what we know of him, we can determine that he was a truly bad man. However, what she did could not have been easy for her. Imagine yourself in a situation today where you had to choose between what would be popular and what would be right. How would you determine the right path from the wrong path and find the courage to do the right thing?

Glossary

Anat: Canaanite goddess of love and war, pictured as the virgin or maiden, and a counterpart and often ally of Baal.

Asherah: Canaanite goddess of the deep, pictured as a serpent, and mother of the Canaanite pantheon of gods.

Ashtartu: Canaanite goddess of maternity, fertility, and intercourse, pictured as the sacred prostitute. Temple prostitution was one of her rites.

augur: one whose job was to read the signs from the entrails of sacrificed animals or the changes in the world around him and to predict the future from what he read.

Baal: The primary Canaanite god during Jael's lifetime, whose symbol was the bull or the calf. He required human sacrifice, especially the sacrifice into fire of all firstborn children.

baqbaq: an earthenware jar used as a carafe.

berit: the covenant between Yahweh and the Israelites that He will be their God, and they will be His people.

El: kindly first main god of the Canaanites, who symbolized the father (and whose symbol was also the bull), and who did not require human sacrifice. He was castrated and supplanted at the head of the pantheon by the bloody, violent Baal.

ezor: a linen loincloth worn only by men.

hagora: a long sash worn over the kuttonet, which wound several times around the waist and both kept the kuttonet in place and added the functionality of pockets. Weapons and tools could be hung from it or tucked into its folds.

halab: goat's milk churned until it contained curds, then served as a drink.

hem'a: butter churned, then boiled to a refined, clear oil. We know it as ghee.

kad: a type of Canaanite or Israelite pottery vessel used for carrying and storing water or grain. The Canaanite versions were often covered with a slip of red clay and painted with black designs of birds, animals, and geometrics in large, bold patterns.

kaddim: plural of *kad*.

kos: drinking cup or drinking bowl.

kuttonet: an ankle-length tunic made of woven wool, worn by both men and women. It draped over the left shoulder, leaving the right shoulder bare. A variant of the kuttonet was the ketonet passim, which had sleeves.

lehem: flat, unleavened bread made in a tannur.

mahabat: a pottery griddle with a slightly concave surface held over an open fire, sometimes on a tripod, and used to parch grain, among other things.

matteh-lehem: a long stick used for reaching into the tannur and pulling out bread once it has finished baking.

mosa: smelter used for melting bronze, brass, gold, and other soft metals, which would then be poured into molds to make jewelry, weapons, tools, and so on.

Mot: the Canaanite god of death and ruler of the underworld.

nazid: the generic term for a vegetarian stew made of grains, legumes, herbs, spices, and fresh vegetables. Its contents would have varied depending upon the season. Nazim was generally eaten by the family sitting around a community pot, sopped up with bread, since silverware didn't exist.

nebel: a pottery wine jar, though the same word originally translated as "wineskin."

no'd: skin container in which goat's milk was stored and curdled.

ostracon (pl. ostraca): a current archeological term for the shards of pottery that were used as writing surfaces. They are common, and seem to have been a writing material of convenience, because pots were fragile and broken pottery was readily available, while shards were cheap and relatively durable.

pleah tahtit: the bottom, fixed stone of the handmill, which had a concave surface onto which grain was poured. Called a "saddle quern" for its resemblance to a saddle.

pelah rekeb: the upper, movable stone of the handmill used for grinding grain. It was rocked over grain in the lower half, and called the "rider" for its resemblance to a man in a saddle.

rehayim: a small stone grain-grinding mill consisting of two parts—the first was the lower stone, or pelah tahtit (which means "saddle quern"), the concave surface in which the grain to be ground was placed; and the second, upper stone or pelah rekeb (which means "rider"), which was pushed back and forth over the grain.

sa'ip: not a veil, but more of a scarf that could be wrapped to cover most of the face.

simla: outer cloak made of a square piece of woven wool, sometimes also held in place by the hagora. At night, it served as a blanket.

sir: wide-mouthed pottery or metal cooking pot.

shar: a prince of the Canaanite people.

tannur: beehive-shaped oven made of fired pottery that was heated by an open fire beneath it and banked around its sides. It was used outdoors to bake both leavened and unleavened bread.

waypassehu: traditional leaping dance used in the worship of the Canaanite god Baal.

yayin: simple fermented grape wine. The Canaanites were well-known for their wines.

Recommended Reading

Bank, Richard D., and Julie Gutin. *The Everything Jewish History & Heritage Book: From Abraham to Zionism, All You Need to Understand the Key Events, People, and Places.* Avon, MA: Adams Media Corporation, 2003.

Cotterell, Arthur, ed. *The Penguin Encyclopedia of Ancient Civilizations.* New York: Penguin, 1989.

Frymer–Kensky, Tikva. *Reading the Women of the Bible: A New Interpretation of Their Stories.* New York: Schocken, 2002.

King, Philip J., and Lawrence E. Stager. *Life in Biblical Israel.* Louisville, KY: Westminster John Knox Press, 2002.

Read on for a preview of
Ann Burton's next Women of the Bible novel

Deborah's Story

Coming from Signet in August 2006

It was through a lush and green garden that I walked, pausing here and there to admire a bloom. Such fragile things, flowers were, and yet they burst forth here as a thousand shofar, trumpeting their colors and beguiling the nose with their sweet scents. Morning dew kissed my toes and birds chirped merrily to me from their perches in the labyrinth of cedar branches overhead.

I loved this place, and came here whenever I could.

Someone had built a fountain in the center of the garden, and that was where I walked now. It was a marvelous thing, carved of polished ivory stone. The water splashing in the basin bubbled up from a hidden spring, so it never ran dry. I scooped some with my hand and brought it to my lips to drink.

"Deborah."

I turned toward the sound. "I am here."

"I have been waiting for you." My love's voice was a warm and wonderful thing that promised laughter and happiness.

I could not see him, but he liked to tease me by hiding. "Where are you?" I left the fountain and began to search for him, smiling as I went. Any moment now, he might jump out and catch me in his arms and whirl me about. "Come out, beloved."

"Deborah." His voice changed. "Deborah, I cannot see you."

The bright sunlight had faded a little, and I looked up to see the sky turning dark with storm clouds. It would rain soon.

"I am here." I pushed aside a tangle of vines. "Come to me and we will go back into the house." If I could find the way to the house. It had grown so dark I could not see the path leading out of the garden anymore.

"I cannot find you." he sounded anxious. "Deborah, hurry."

Lightning slashed across the black clouds, and wind rushed through the garden to tear at my clothes. I threw up my hands as leaves pelted my face. "I must leave you now. Take shelter."

"Deborah, do not go!"

I turned this way and that, trying to avoid being lashed by the waving branches of the trees. Flowers flew away on the wind, torn from their stems. The light was gone, the sun swallowed by the storm, and I reached out my hand to feel my way.

A hole appeared a few feet away from me, jagged-edged and black as pitch.

A sharp pain struck my shoulder, and I cried out as I fell. I did not want to leave the garden, for it was the only place I felt safe, but I would die if I stayed. "Farewell," I sobbed, crawling toward the ugly scar in the ground. "Farewell, my love."

"Deborah, come back! I will get you to safety! I will get—"

Get.

Get up.

"Do your ears not work?" Something slammed into my shoulder again. "Get up, you lazy slut."

The hard kick knocked me over, so that I lay facedown in the straw. I bit back another cry and quickly curled over, pushing myself up onto my knees.

Ybyon stood over me, his broad face a mask of ugly shadows, his eyes narrow with contempt. "On your feet, girl."

The corner of the barn where I slept was silent, and only the light from the hanging lamp the master carried illuminated the darkness. The others who slumbered next to me in the straw were already gone; I had slept too long again.

"Forgive me, Master," I begged as I stood and tugged my tunic down over my thighs. It hung loosely, for it had once belonged to one of the kitchen wenches. I was given it when it became too stained and threadbare for her to wear. That it was too large did not matter to me. It covered my body, and gave me a little warmth at night when I slept.

Ybyon paused, as if deciding whether to kick me again. "Get to work." He turned and stalked out to the pens.

Because it was so near dawn, I did not dare leave the barn and go to the kitchens for my bread. Instead I retrieved my pan from where it hung on the wall and carried it to the first stall. The old, bad-tempered spotted goat kept there was eating a pile of scraps from the kitchen refuse heap, and bleated her annoyance as I crouched beside her.

I said nothing when she butted my aching shoulder with her head. I milked her quickly and whisked the pan from beneath her before she could kick it over with her hooves. Her milk warmed the pan and floated, thick and foamy around the edges. I looked from side to side and then bent my head to drink a mouthful before I carried the pan out of the stall.

"Deborah." Meji came and took the pan from me, and looked about before he said in a whisper, "Sorry. I tried to wake you but you would not move, and then Hlagor shouted for me."

"It matters not." That I had slept too long on a morning that I knew Ybyon would come to inspect the barns and stables was my fault. I had sat up alone last night, watching stars shoot across the sky, when I should have been sleeping. I heard the master's voice drawing close and touched Meji's thin arm before I hurried out to the pens.

Ybyon owned five hundred sheep and two hundred goats, as well as some cows, mule, oxen and onagers. One of his businesses was the buying and selling of beasts, so the number occupying the pens and stalls constantly changed. My morning task was to check the sheep pens and see that no lambs had been dropped or injured during the night. In winter I hated going into the pens, for I always found too many of the early births dead of cold or being trampled. Now it was almost spring, I would have to be more vigilant, for the fat ewes would begin dropping their lambs by the dozen each night.

The sheep pen smelled much worse than the barn, and the ground beneath my bare feet was slick with manure. Many of the sheep needed their hooves cut back and cleaned out, for they had grown over, but that would not be done until they were sold. Their wool was thick and greasy to the touch, and their narrow, dark heads turned to look at me as I waded through them.

I saw one of the ewes by the fence, standing as far from the herd as she could manage in the confines of the pen. A stringy, wet mass hanging from beneath her chubby tail, the afterbirth from her dropping the lamb that lay curled on the ground beneath her.

The lamb was at suck, and the ewe lowered her

head as I approached, but I did not disturb them. If I tried to take the lamb now the ewe would charge me. Instead I watched the little one have his first meal. I had never known my own mother, so such things drew me.

"Girl!" Ybyon strode toward me, driving the sheep out of his way. "Why do you idle there?"

I bowed my head. "It is a new lamb, Master."

"Yes, yes, I can see that." He clouted the side of my head with his fist. "Why do you not carry it to the lamb pen?"

I cringed and pressed my fingers to my throbbing ear. "It is nursing, Master."

Ybon reached down, tore the lamb from its mother and shoved it into my arms. "Now it is not. Take it."

The ewe reacted strongly to this intrusion by charging Ybyon. The master caught her by the neck and spun around, flinging her into the fence. She lay there, stunned and unmoving.

"If she does not rise to go to graze, have one of the shepherds cut her throat," Ybyon told me before he strode out of the pen.

"Yes, Master." I cuddled the bleating lamb close to my chest. I did not dare take him back to his mother to try to rouse her. I never disobeyed Ybyon or questioned what he wished done with his property. No matter how cruel or unfair his orders were, I always carried them out.

I did this because I, too, was Ybyon's property—

his slave, from the moment of my birth, just as my mother had been. If I did not do exactly what my master said, he would not send for one of the shepherds to cut my throat.

He would do it himself. As he had when he killed my mother.